DOOMS DAY

Dedicated
To Our Children

PREFACE

Asteroid Day 30 June
Asteroid Day is a global awareness campaign where people from around the world come together to learn about asteroids, the impact hazard they may pose and what we can do to protect our planet, families, communities and future generations from future asteroid impacts. Asteroid Day is held each year on the anniversary of the largest impact in recent history, the 1908 Tunguska event in Siberia on 30 June.

DOOMS DAY

Vinod Kumar Mishra

PARTRIDGE

To order additional copies of this book, contact
Partridge India
000 800 10062 62
orders.india@partridgepublishing.com

www.partridgepublishing.com/india

CONTENTS

INTRODUCTION

N ow adays, every school children knows about the origin of Planets and Earth. They also know about the progress made in the field of science and technology but the dark side of this development is unknown to them. The Global Warming and misuse of Atomic Weapons is a threat that can not be avoided. Mother Nature has its own course of Action which we see in untimely floods, hail storm, lend slides, volcano, and other calamities. The scientist believe that as in past, in future after ten or twenty years An Asteroid big enough to destroy living beings, may strike on Earth. In our solar system between Mars and Jupiter, there is an Astroid Belt where more than ninety thousands small and big stony Asteroids are traveling around. When they collide with each other they change direction and are attracted by other planets gravity. It is believed that some four millions years back when a ten km. wide Asteroid hit the Earth, near mexico peninsula the heatwaves, fire and smoke was so dense that the whole Earth was engulfed in darkness for months resulting which Dynosours became extinct. Other example can be seen in Moon and at Earth where great craters were made by them in past. Over two hundreds of these craters have been discovered in various locations of earth. Scientists are developing various means to divert or destroy the Astroid in Space. It is a complececed manouver and needs months tharough planning. They may succeed. But what will happen if they failed to divert the Asteroid's course or destroy it completely, it seems to be important. On 21 June 2002 when I was fast sleep, I had a dream that An Asteroid had striked the Earth creating destruction everywhere. I was awoken but thought it to be a Dream only. I was astonished to see in the morning news papers that an Astroid had passd by the Earth on 14th June in a great speed of which nobody knew earlier. I was in shocke. Only few people around the world seemed to be worried. This made me think that some serious planning should be done to make general people aware of it, if that type of catastrophy struck again in future. The incident kept me worried for some days. I had to do something but what? It was a question that has to be answerd. A thought came into my mind that I should write about it in a way people will be aware of the life threatening danger. As the story was based on facts not fiction, it was easy to write if you made yourself a character in the Act.. I made characters, place, time and started writing it. Six young boys and girls of different nationalities meet by coincidence and with love, affection, dedication, struggle to survive the deep impact of "Dragon" the Asteroid, which was going to colide with the Earth.

You will wonder as to how simple things of day to day life, people forget. These simple things can make difference between life and death. There is every answer of your questions as How, Why, What. I have not written this Novel to frighten you but to make you, aware of danger, our generation may face in future. If you want our children, to survive in future disasters. If you want to feel the Terror of the happenings, klick on to Asteroids on Internet for detailed information. This is for common man and woman who have no access to Internet or have no time to think between the strugle of bread and butter. You will agree with me that whatever I have written, will thrill you to the extent that you are bound to act accordingly if the time came. You would like to be in one of the six survivers who will save the Earth from Human species extinction.

With due respect.
VinodMishra
Sadar Bazar, Bilaspur C.G.
Mobile- 919425536550

Main Characters:-

1 - **Amitabh**
2 - **Gauri**
3 - **Manish**
4 - **Rajkumar**
5 - **Tanya**
6 - **Juli**
7 - **Sukhiya & Yuri Terishkov.**

Place:- Rampur Distt. Jaipur, Rajasthan. INDIA

CHAPTER 1

AMITABH

1ST November 2024/ 2050

It was half passed three and I was sitting under a tree beside teashop, dejected but hopeful that I should do something instead of spending time here and there walking around Delhi. The event was World Tradefair which was to be inougurated on 14th November at Delhi the capital of India. It was an yearly event and all developing countries took part in it, with their technical progress and know how. The workers had already been engaged and were busy inside the Gate in various jobs. But alas I was sitting idle and hoping to hapen something which will revive my energy from boredom. Beside, gate number, three, four loaded trucks were waiting for gate pass. This was my third day in Delhi looking for any job, to pass one and half month before my previous employer called me for the construction of Fertilizer Factory at Chhattisgarh. I was in two minds, either I should accept any job which came by or I should go back to Rampur my native place. Oriental Febricater, where I worked for two years, have given me a hope that sooner or later I will achieve my goal of a successful engineer, doing better in life. Situated at Gudgaon, Oriental Fabricater were top leading company of India were busy in establishing big industrial units. They were installing various units in different parts of India. The works were done on contract basis to complete it on the given time. The sailery was good with other facilities. Just fifteen days back we had completed the work of an Oil Refinery at Gujrat in record time. We were being told that another construction work of Fertilizer Factory at Chhattisgarh will be starting soon and we should be ready for it but instead, we along with hundred fifty other co-workers, were shocked to learn of being relieved from duties till further orders. We were told that we will have to wait for another five six months when Oriental Fabricators got clearance from Bitco Corporation, the American Company which were to erect Fertilizer Plant at Chhattisgarh. Bitco Corporation were experts in making fertilizer, from coal and were doing several erections through out the world. Oriental were negotiating with them, since long until they had an agreement with them. The work had to start within six months, but something unusual happened and Bitco Corporation withholded the commitioning of the plant for six months.

In India being an agriculture country, this was not unusual, state governments made Plans and start the work but before they are completed another party comes into power in the state and they made their own planning, stopping the previous works. Crores of rupees spent were misused like this. In 1947 India got its independence from British rule and started the work of progress in different fields. Previously it was all write for forty years then, when no single party got mejority, coliation government were formed in Center and everything became upside down. Politics became a source of income. Nationality was forgotten, vote politics began, criminals became more powerful and by mussle power got elected in Loksabha. People got fed up with the mess they had created and in the last century the congress rule was over and the opposition party came into power. A new beginning started to take shape, the News Papers and TV which were before mouth piece of political parties began to support and advocate what should be done for the development of country. The production increased in every field, the industries which were running in loss began to show profit, everywhere a hope of fulfillment was gaining but that was not so with me. Just I had come from Gujrat where I was working as a mechanical engineer in an oil refinery. Next job was at Chhattisgarh, where my employer Oriental Febricater was going to build a Fertilizer Factory, under an American Company Bitco Corporation. An agreement has already been made and the work of installation was to be started in six months. At Gujrat refinery, we had completed the job at record time, fifteen days earlier, we had to move to Chhattisgarh for our next commitment but something unusual happened. The inauguration of Fertilizer Factory at Chhattisgarh has already been done but I with hundred fifty other workers were asked to wait for another six months when they received a green signal from Bitco Corporation. This was unusual but to pass the time I was here at Delhi looking for any temporary job. Luckily here at Delhi, World Trade Fare, an Yearly event was being inaugurated on November Fourtinth, hence too many companies were busy in erection of their stalls and I was sitting under a tree beside a Tea shop, looking for any job that will keep me busy, till I was called back from my previous employer. Some of my coligues were already engaged inside in manual job but being an engineer I had to wait for something, as per my choice, I was sitting here beside a teashop from nine in the morning to evening at five to hapen something. If I get a prestigious job I will stay here otherwise, I will have to go back to my native place Rampur. I was feeling at my bones that this is the place where my stars will shine again and will direct me, to new destiny, hence I checked myself for going back to Rampur where my little sister Gauri was waiting alone, hoping, her brother Amitabh will achieve his goal of success. Being an elder brother I had the responsibility of Father and she was acting as a Mother because both my parents died unexpectedly. Time has change, unwillingly I was sitting here at Delhi, beside a teashop three hundred km. away from Rampur.

Suddenly I came to my senses and began to hear sound of traffic on the road and murmur of cold air, birds singing on trees. I heard an one sided argument going between four sardar truck drivers and a middle aged gentle man, nearby four heavily loaded sixteen wheeler trucks were parked. They were coming towards teashop arguing. I stood up and advanced towards them. Perhaps my apearence of, fair complexion, moderately dressed in Denim jeens, black swetar, gold framed spectecals has attracted them, An elderly sardar cried saheb ji, we are waiting here since morning, this gentel man came to receive us, went back but again came back without any labours to unload the truck. Says about some agreement but does nothing. We have to go to Ludhiyana to marrow and if we do not move before seven in the morning, we will be forced to stay here because of road block. We don't want any halting charge, the trucks must be unloaded before morning. Please convey our problem to this gentleman. I assured him that I will do my best to solve the problem. Uptill now the person addressed was standing were quietly, when sardarji finished talking, he turned to me and said Namaste ji, my name is Yuri Terishkov, I look after the exhibitions held around the world, directed by my government, will you please help me. He gave me some papers. The papers were of an agreement between Ayangar & co.of Benglore and Russian trade promotion buroe by which Ayangaar & co. has to dismental, transport and erect a Dome like structure at Benglore, Bombay and Delhi on payment of Rs. Fifty thousand each. A penalty of Rs. Ten thousand was to be imposed if the work was not completed in time. Mr. Terishkov further said that his assistant, who looked after the commissioning got infected by Maleriya, was bed ridden at Bombay, hence he has to look after the commissioning of Dome here at Delhi. He is not familiar with the job as his assistant did this in past. He could not arrange the labours to unload the trucks. He is ready to pay all the charges. Nobody at Ayangar & co. is responding to his call. His worried face was telling all the problems he was facing. Now I had to take the decision. Rs. Ten thousand for unloading the trucks at site was a good offer. The question was wather in short notice, can I arrange the labours and a Crane to unload the trucks before seven in the morning. My only hope depended on my fellow workers who were working inside the exhibition ground. I remembered the saying that success comes to those who dare and act, it seldom goes to timid. On impulse I turned towords Mr. Terishkov and said O.K sir I will get it done. He seemed relieved but said he knew it. Now it was my turn to be surprised. I said sir how do you knew. He directed his finger towords my shirt pocket where Oriental Febricaters golden embroiderd badge was shining, which I had forgotten to remove. Luck has given me second opportunity unexpectedly. When I told the truck drivers the good news, they began to dance with relief. Time was the utmost important. We all moved to the Administrative office where checking all the papers, gate passes were given to truck drivers and my credentials were checked, Name- Amitabh Sharma s/o Shri Rameshvar Sharma, Height -5.10, Profession – Contractor, Employers Name – Mr. Yuri Terishkov, Trade promotion Buro of Russian Federetion. After three long days of waiting, I got something to do.

On Delhi Mathura road, near old fort, on Pragati maidan, country's first Prime Minister Sri Jawaharlal Nehru had inaugurated on 14th Nov. 1950 World Trade Fare. Every year many developed countries took part in it, demonstrating their products to increase their sale. For fourteen days, thousands of people and prospective customers visited various pavelians to fulfill their enquiries. Along with Mr. Terishkov I enterd the exhibition ground. Beside Administrative office there was a Board where detailed map of various halls and their direction was shown. A little distance away, in a beautifull garden workers were busy in decorating with different type of flowers. Everywhere workers were busy in installation doing various jobs. Mr. Terishkov took me to an open rectangular ground some two hundred meters away. He opened a detailed map of the road and showed me where all the goods were to be unloded. Time was running very fast so I borrowed his car and proceeded towards where maximum work was in progress to engage some labours who will do the job in overtime. I was hoping to meet some of my fellow workers who were already engaged there. It was like searching a needle on a stack of Hay but I had to try. I moved around but could not find anyone. I stopped the car in front of

L.G pavelian to phone my previous aquented contracters, when a worker who was painting flagpole hailed me, saying Namaste Chhote Saab. I was surprised, he was none other than Jagdish my fellow worker at Gujrat. I approched him hopefully and told my problem. He became glad and called his two fellow workers. Jagdish told me that this was their last day of working there and are ready to do the overtime on payment of Rs. four hundred each. I asked him about a Crane that will be needed to unload the truck, he took me to the back gate of exhibition ground, where many Cranes were parked. I was able to get Batra;s Crane on payment of Rs, three thousand. Relieved I left one worker with the crane and gave direction of Russiyan site. Mr. Terishkov was anxiously waiting, when we reached back. When I told him about the crane and workers I have arranged, he seemed to be relieved. By this time all the four trucks had arrived and were parked beside the side road. He instructed the workers to unload two round heavy bundels from a truck and within thirty minutes got assembled one Tent near the back wall and were furnished with cots, table, chair and other things necessary for residing. He further showed me the spot where all the crates were to be unloaded. This done, he gave me his hotel Rajdoot's address, phone number and said that he will come back after some time.

When the crane arrived, I instructed the oprater to lift the big crate by fastning steel ropes on both sides of the crate. I did not know the weight of the big crate so I was worried but when it was lifted easily I gave a sigh of relief. With the help of Jagdish and his coworkers, the crate was deposited on the site. I told the truck drivers to go and enjoy their meals at canteen. They rejoicely went away. Gradualy in three hours all the crates and boxes were unloaded and were put in between two tents, as desired by Mr. Terishkov. It was already nine o clock so I asked Jagdish and his friends to come in the morning for payment. Once again I checked all the crates and boxes with the list and found them all correct but feeling a bit tired. It was getting cold so I put on my sweater and went inside the tent to rest. It was a beautifull tent with red and white strips. To paas the time, I took out a Novel from my backpack and sitting on an easy chair started reading it, At about elevon Mr. Terishkov arrived. He looked relieved and congratulated me in completing the job in a short time. He had brought with him some cakes and coffee which I enjoyed very well because I had not eaten anything since evening. He paid cash to the truck drivers. Mr. Terishkov than advised me to rest in the tent since it was getting late in the night and said that he will come in the morning to discuss his future plans. I undressed and lied down on the bed to sleep which will not come, instead my mind went back to dreaming the events for back to my childhood and towords my little beloved sister Gauri.

I was awakened by my little sister Gaory calling me several times to answer her question which she did not know. I knew that unless I did not answered her query she will not be satisfied. She asked me that she knew how Solar and Moon eclipse happen but in between Earth and Sun there were two more Planets Mercury and Venus, than why did not they formed Eclipse like Sun and Moon. At first I was taken abeck, a child studying in eight standard asking this type of a question surprised me. I knew that Mercury was around six crore and Venus eleven crore km. away from Sun and were small in size comparatively with Earth but Moon was only Five Lakhs km. from Earth which plays the role of Eclipse. I looked at Gauri's mischievius look and instantly understood that she was testing me. I began to laugh and asked did.nt she knew the answer? She replied joyfully that nobody in her class knew the answer except herself. she only was testing me. I was relieved to hear this. I was studying in class twelve and next year I had to take admission in Enginiering college. Two of my classmetes Manish and Rajkumar were my best friends. Manish was the son of Shri Sheodulare Dubey, our neighbour and Rajkumar was the son of shri Chandrabhan singh Rathore, a wellknown richman of Rampur. From eighth standard we were good friends and stood togather everywhere. We were called Three Musketiers. My brain, Manish's strength and Rajkumar's egileness made a good combination, that people outside and students in school feard but we never misused it. Manish was healthy and participated in wresling and Boxing while Rajkumar nicknamed as Raju was the captain of Badminton team. I was topper in studies so at exam time both Manish and Raju took my help. Whenever Raju went to Jaipur he always took us with him to enjoy. Manish and father, were great friend. They both had come from Shahpur village of unnav dist. u.p. to earn their living togather. Doing several jobs they had purchased agriculture land near Ramgadhi fort and settlled in Rampur. Previously they earned a lot but uncertainty of rain and increasing cost of labour had forced them to do something else and hence Dubey uncle had opened a grain shop and my father became a science teacher in school. Every Sunday, at noon, we three friends and Gauri played cards. chaupad and ceramboard but in winter and summer holidays, we went to agriculture farm which was eight km. away on bycycles. Adjoining to farm there was a huge tank and beside it a narrow lane which went upto the fort. Before farm on left side of the road there was a small hill and on top of the hill a small temple of GodessDurga. We always stopped at the bottam of the hill, leaving bycycles there, at a signal started climbing the hill in competeion. Joking and teasing we ran to be first but Gauri always left us behind. After worshipping the Godess we rested there sometime than ascending the hill came to farm. Bathing in the tank and enjoying our lunch we climbed upto the fort and surveyed the surroundings playing and joking. Those were the golden days of our childhood. My final exam was over and science practial were in progress when suddenly a fire broke out in the lab, Father saved all the students but the fuming gases and broken glass injured him so much that before he could be taken to hospital he died on the spot. All were stunned. We could not do any thing, our green pasture of hope was destroyed in a second. A huge crowd of people and students gathered in his funeral to give him homage. We were worried for mother as she was a heart patient but she took it bravely consoling herself, that father saved all the students. We all wept together. Financialy it was a great blow to us, agriculture income was not sufficient to meat the household expanses. Dubey uncle was in a shock but he consoled mother and promised to help us in every possile way. Gauri was very much attached to father but suddenly she took the charge of house, attending mother all the time and doing house jobs. I tried to get a job in Rampur but who will give a freshar boy of sixteen years who knows nothing. I rememberd my father's saying that no work is small, keep yourselves busy, it is better to do a honrary work than sit idle. Asking my mother that I had got a Job at Bhilwada, started going there in morning and came back at night. Bhilwada was an insustrial city eighty km. away. As helper I started learning as mason.carpentar blacksmith, electrician etc. whatever came in that time to earn money. It continued for six months. In the meantime, we all friends were seprated. Manish went to Bikaner Agriculture college and Rajkumar, somewhere at west Bengal to Mountainiering college. Gauri was left alone in Rampur to look after mother. She was with mother all the time. Dubey uncle as promised did help us a lot. My mother was a Sanskrit Graduate so sympathizing with her she was given an appointment as a Sanskrit teacher in the school. Provident fund of my father was also releasd soon. Dubey uncle's effort I was able to get admission in Jaipur Eng, college on merit grounds. Gauri started going to school with mother as usual and life became easier. Time cures all the wounds. Leaving sarrow aside mother started taking intrest in every field. Every fortnight with Gauri she went to farm and began to supervise the crop production. Whenever I came to Rampur on holidays we tried to follow our old routine. In my absence a fatefull incident happened. Manish had come back to Rampur leaving his studies of agriculture and was busy in developing his farm production by the knowledge he had gained in two years. By producing twice he had surprised Dubey uncle so he had closed his grain shop and gave full help to Manish. One day while searching their bull in forest, a serpent bited Dubey uncle and by the time he was taken to hospital, it was too late and he died. Manish was left alone. It was a severe blow. Dubey uncle were our guardian now Manish too became alone. I rushed to Rampur and consoled Manish in every way possible. After her first shock mother had gained confidence by this time, so she called Manish and assured him that from now on she would look after Manish also and to confirm she gave the responsibility of her agriculture land to Manish. She accompnied Manish to farm and advised him to erect a tubewell of which she will take bank guarantee. Thus she managed to encourage Manish in forgetting his loneliness. He took his meals with mother and Gauri and only at night went to his house. Sukhiya chachi too became our family member doing various household jobs and gradualy all became normal. Completeing my final studies, on first May evening when I reached Rampur, Mother and Gauri embraced me shading tears of happyness.. It was an accomplishment achieved in hard times, so we all went to our worshiping place and said our prayers, like we did in past. We were thankfull to God who had helped us to recover fast at the time of distress. At the same time Manish entered the house, from the farm, with vegitables in a bag and seeing me rushed to meet and embraced me saying now we both will face the challange of life strongly. He was dressed in jeans and T shirt and looked smart and strong. I was pleased to look at his strong phisic, farm duties had done good to him. Both mother and Gauri were smiling, seeing us entangled in arms affectionately. Now Gauri invited both of us in the kitchen where she had prepared Poteto Paratha for this occasion. Sukhiya chachi was busy in making chatny. Seeing me she looked happy and said I looked starved and had become thinner. She said I should stay here for some time and gain some strength before doing anything. Sukhiya chachi now had become a family member, she did all the housework and slept in Manish house at night. Manish everyday at eight in the morning used to go to the farm taking his tiffin and returned at evening only. Every night he dined with mother before going home. Now we all dined togather and after that in mother's room talked and enjoyed our future plans. Gauri said that she had learned

computer and wanted to do MCA. She requested me to buy
her a computer when ever I got an appointment and a
telephone to be in touch with me and her friends which were
growing in number. I was relaxed till the Exam results were
declared and after that a search for service will start, which
was not easy as the competeion in unemployment was
tremendous with growing population. In between talks we
decided to visit our farm next morning to boost up our
forgotten childhood adventures.

It was seven in the morning when we three started on
our cycles to farm which was eight km. away. Our village had
now developed into a town with Banks, Hotels, computer's
cafe etc. Small factories. dairy, chicken farm had opened
on right side of the road. Left side the small hill continued
upto Ahmadabad highway. Near our farm at the bottom of
the hill there was a big Banyan tree with plateform where
people rested for a while. Reaching there we kept our cycles
beside and at a nod started climbing the hill as we did in
the past many times. At first I was ahead than Gauri passed
me but before reaching at the top Manish took the lead and
reached at the temple. Gauri was clapping merily, it looked
as if she had got back her childhood again.. I was exahsted
and understood that I will have to work hard to improve
my stamina. After resting a while I looked around and
felt that I was looking the sarroundings for the first time
in life. The murmur of cold clean air was electrifying the
body and soul. I began to feel that if I had wings, I will fly
to the sky. We were at the height of hundred fifty feet on
the hill which was on the south east of Rajasthan. Below on
east side, a vast green landscape with trees, garden and crop
fields looked beautiful. The hill itself gradualy sloped upto
a km. to Rampur town which was seven km. away. West

side below the winding road joined the Delhi Ahmadabad highway. Hundred meters away sarrounded by trees, must be our farm beside a huge Tank. Connected to the tank, the old Ramgadhi fort looked like a scene painted in canvas. Behind the fort, small hills continued upto for away Aravali Mountain. At south side in between hills Banasriver flowed to join the sacred Yamuna River. This plateu was thousand feet above the sea level sarounded by Luniriver on north near Jaipur, Banas river, at south and for away in UP by Yamuna river on east, a very fertile land indeed. As I rememberd our farm was near the tank behind a stony dump which I could not see and was confused. I asked Manish about it who said it was in the same place beside tank. Gauri came to my help and directed me to a small house and garden sarrounded by trees. She said bhaiya, Manish had been doing all practicals of agriculture college here. Leaving his college in two years, remaining two years of his practicals he had completed here only. I looked towords Manish who was turning his eyes from me. Surprised I congratulated Manish on this but he answered that whatever he has done, were planed by Badi Maa and Gauri. I had tried my best to fulfill it. I was successfull or not you had to decide, I embraced him and said come on now we are getting late and should go to the farm as well. Slowly we came down from the hill and taking our cycles proceded about hundred meters, towords agriculture farm, It was ten feet upwords from the road. Closing the wooden gate we enterd inside. There was a flatend sqared space coverd with green grass where the stony dump used to be. In all side flower and fruit plantation had been done. A tubewell was installed within a distance from the tank which was full of water. Backside of the space a two room small house was made. There was enough space behind the house for putting haystock. A bullock cart was kept beside the cattleshade. To put grains a Kothi was built inside the house. A narrowlane divided the tank and the fields of ractengular shape spread upto the fence for behind. The narrowlane went upto the fort which was two hundred meters away. I was pleasd to look the efforts made by Manish in two years. I asked Manish about the stoni dump which was there. Manish explained that he needed extra space for growing crop. By this time the road was being brodend and the contracter needed stones for it, which he was to dig from the hill, I suggested him to dig stones from our stony dump. He did the same and we both were pleasd in removing the stony dump. The small stones left, I used in making pavement between our fields. He further said that he was taking three crops per year and had cleard the Bank loan. On an Acre of land he had made a nursery for his experiments learned in college. All the accounting and production management, he had done this with the help and guidence of Gauri which she had learned from Internet. He praised Gauri for her knowledge and intrest in every field. He further said that he was surprisd for Gauri's imagination and logical approch in searching every problem. It looks as if she had a Computer fitted in her brain. Closing my eyes I did all this work. I had engaged two labours also. The good quality production is sold immediately. We were talking all this when Gauri called that she had arranged the food in between two wooden beds and we should enjoy it washing our hands at the tubewell. By this time we were feeling hungry so enjoyed Puri Paratha heartly. When we started to come back Manish asked, AmitDa you had seen all this without any comment now suggest something, which you feel, had to be done more. By complementing Manish I said Manish you have done a great job here and as per my advice if you purchase two cows, it will be more profitable. You had enough fodder for them and cowdung you will get, will produce gas for cooking and good manure for the fields. We were walking back to our cycles when suddenly they stopped and Gauri exclaimed oh Bhaiya how she could not think of such a small thing. Realy you are a genious. You have surpassed us in a step. We laughd aloud. Evening was approching so we came back joking and teasing each other.

At the end of June, exam results were declared. I was successfull in geting merits. Now the second face of waiting began, apply for a job, attend interview and hope for the best. Whenever I was at home, went to the farm with Manish and worked four hours in the morning.. Every Sunday, we climbed the hill as usual and enjoyed. In spare time did all sorts of repairing in house and farm. Manish had colected all sorts of applainces used in masonary, carpenting, farming and chakiya, dhenki etc. needed as per requirment. In one shade, was experimenting Mashroom cultivation. He was a good worker lacking only in managemnt. I planned first in paper than helped him in materialising in practice. Within two months, all completed, we congratulated each other on our fulfilment. Our childhood friendship had become now an unbreakable bond of brotherhood. Twice I had gone for interview with no luck because I wanted the job nearby. To look for vacancies in newspaper had become my daily routine. November came and a good crop had florishd the market resulting rush of byers. We celibrated Diwali festival ostentaliously. On Bhaiduj day when Gauri returned from computer classes she gave me a vacancy enquiry collected from Internet. It was a walk in interview, for two mechanical engineers. Posts were temporary. Working place, all India.

Payment, as per qualification. My father used to say it is better to do an honrary job than sitting idle. Atleast you will learn something. This saying has made me a Jack of all trades. The ade was from Oriental Fabricaters Gudgaon Delhi at Regency Hotel on seventh December at two clock.

On sixth morning I proceeded by bus to Delhi, reaching at seven in the evening and spent the night at a small hotel in Pahadgunj. Next day at twelve, fully prepared with my credentials took a light breakfast and reached Regency Hotel at one thirty sharp. Taking guidence from the reception I reached room no. six two two on sixth floor by climbing the stairs. Nine competeters were already sitting there. Beside Orient Fabricater's banner, two clerks were busy in sorting papers. They took down my name, addresse and said to wait for his call. The winter season was at its peak but a tension prevailed in the room. Out of nine present four looked seniaurs who were in suit and remaining freshers like me in shirt paint. I wore Jeans and T shirt. Morning Puja was in my daily routine and always put a chandan Tika on my forhead as mother taught us. Nobody was talking much. Everybody looked tense. At two o clock the bell rang and the clerk began to call one by one to go inside where the interviewer sat. Everybody was asked to sit back on his chair after the interview, I was the last one to go inside at about three o clock. Though the room was airconditioned I was peraspiring. Wiping it I enterd the room. Behind a big table interviewee sat. I greeted them respectfully and sat down on the front chair. They saw my credentials and asked three four questionson on various subjects which I answered promptly. They knew that I had no experience as a freshar but asked what payment I will accept. I replied that it is upto them to decide after seeing my work. Afterwords the clerk announced that we all have to pass one hurdle of fitness. One of the clerks, took us down to the ground floor and said that one by one, we all have to climb the stairs upto sixth floor where the time we took in ascending, will be recorded, We all were given a card on which the time was to be rcorded. By recording the time the clerk sent us one by one to sixth floor. The event completed, we were given tea and snaks and informed that the selected candidate will be informed by post in time. At first I was astonished in doing this physical type of interview but than I understood the importance. In keen competetion every fast growing company had to get maximum output from their employies and to achieve that physical fitness was a must. Hoping for the best I reached back to Rampur next morning at seven o clock. Mother, Gauri and Manish were anxiously waiting for me. They wanted to know all about the interview. In between our breakfast I repeated all that had happened in detail. Hearing all this Gauri began to dance and said Bhaiya I know that you will be selected definately. She further said that in throat cutting competetion which company gets more output in less workers will make profit that is why expert interviewer are being appointed. As you have traveled all night you must be exahsted so go to pujaghar and take blessings from God and mother before you take rest.

From next day, old routine of morning at farm and evening at library started again. Life seemed to be stand still. The day of full moon Purnima I still remember very much. Each month at Purnima, my mother celibrated it with traditional Puja. After taking morning bath we all collected at mother's room in front of a small temple in which the Idol of God Bramha, Vishnu and Mahesh were worshiped by mother daily. On this day she used to make, by rice flour a symbolic nine planets, ahead a water filld jar. On top of that a small cupfull of pure ghee, in between a candle was lightened. Ahead she put Shri Ganesh ji's replica and after doing all this she started worshiping saying sanskrit prayers. She offered fruits and sweets to all Gods and planets. During Arati we rang bells and horn, joining mother in prayers. But on this particular day when the worshipping was completed and prasad of sweets fruits and panchamrit were being distributed, Sukhiya chachi brought a postal envelop and gave it to Gauri. Seeing the envelope Gauri immediately put it on the steps of God and joyfuly declared that Bhaiya on this holy occasion, in this envelope, there would not be any other news but your selection and joining letter. Opening it I found that Oriental Fabricaters had invited me to join and report at Gudgaon factory for two months apprenticeship on Rs twenty thousand per month and completing that on Rs. forty thousand per month as regular pay. Mother had happy tears in her eyes when I touched her feet for blessing. Gauri and Manish embraced me. All were glad that I was selected for the job but I will have to go to Gudgaon leaving them alone saddend them. One week passed in my preparation. The daily routine had to be changed accordingly in my absence. It was decided that in the morning Manish will accompany mother to the school and afterwords go to farm, returning in the evening he will attend other house jobs. Gauri will do her college education privately studying at home. She will bring mother from school and after that will go to computer classes. Sukhiya chachi as usual will look after house duties and help mother. This all arranged I left for Gudgaon on thirty first December and reported my presence at Oriental Fabricater's office. Mr Vasudevan who had taken my interview, informed me that the contract was for two years, after two months training there, I was to go to Sanad, where an oil refinery was being erected. Free lodging, dining and medical facilities I will enjoy with other officers and workers. After two months vigarous training of welding, cutting, bending, polishing and other theory classes made me a perfect enginer. Before going to Sanad at Gujrat I went to Rampur on five days preparation leave. Mother, Gauri and Manish greeted me heartly and wanted to know my experience which I narrated briefely. I was glad to see that they were doing well. We spent maximum time togather by chit chating and playing indoor games. One day I went to the farm. Manish had purchased two cows and pups. Wheat crop was thriving. Seeing all this I understood that everything will be fine in my absence. On first April I joined my duties as assistant engineer in Sanad oil refinary. I lived in bechlor quarters, which was near construction site with other officers. Rising at six o clock in the morning, after toilet and bathing, did Yoga and Puja for fifteen minutes, dressing went to dining hall for breakfast. and at the hoot of Siren at eight o clock, reached on work site. I had eight fitters and three helpers under me and two units of assembling to supervise. Each day Mr. Vasudevan our immediate boss gave us the blueprint of work that had to be done. We had to go to the store and fetch required machines, valves and pipes of all sizes. With the help of chain pullys and trollys, we were busy all the time. At lunch time of an hour we rested a bit and were busy again. Mr. Vasudevan knew every worker by name and came twice to supervise and gave direction if any problem we faced. My co-woerkers addresed me as chhote saab or pandit ji as I had a chandan Tika on my forhead. On holiday we all went to the seaside where a big jetty was being constructed to berth big Oil

Tankers. For the first time, I was thrilled to look at the sea and enjoyed a boat ride. On fifteenth August holiday we went to Surat city for shopping and sight seeing. Passing by a showroom I saw life jackets and waterproof goggles. As I did not knew swimming on impulse I purchased three sets for Manish, Gauri and myself. Returning back the old routine of work started again. Within six months first face of construction and erection was completed. I took seven days leave for Diwali festival, reached Bhilwada by train and by Bus to Rampur. Both Manish and Gauri received me at the Bus station. I looked at Gauri, a five feet six inches heighted girl with big eyes, long hairs, fair complexond smiling beauty, happy tears in her eyes, she embraced me, complaining that I should come very often. For the first time I felt that she had become matured leaving her childhood behind. She further complained that she had completed computer course and feeling lonely was bord at home either I should by her a computer or I should get married so that my wife will give her company. I kissed her on forehead and promised to do anything she required. At home mother was glad to see me, her health was good but she became tired soon. We celebrated Diwali festival heartly and enjoyed very well. One day between lunch I asked mother that Gauri had come of age and she should be married soon. Mother convinced me that she already had selected groom for Gauri and she would like to get married Gauri and afterwords to me as early as possible. The vacation over I was busy again in the factory. Second face of work erecting storage tank in many numbers were being built. I was very popular with my fellow workers as I treated them as equals and helped them in every way. Next year by the end of June three fourth of the was completed and electrical work was in progress when on nineth July I received a phone call from Gauri that while coming back from school mother got weted by unexpected rains. She had fever and was asking for me. I rushed and reached Rampur next day. Seeing me mother had tears in eyes. I was shocked to see mother's condition. In twenty four hours fever she became so weak that she could not sit herself. I called specilist doctor from Jaipur. He declared that mother had devloped Nimoniya and is not good for heart patient. He prescribed medicines for that. Except praying to God we were unable to do anything. I, Manish and Gauri took turns, one by one to attend and help mother in any way possible. Next day she seemed to feel better. When Manish had gone to market to bring medicine mother called me and Gauri near her and said that she wanted to tell us something we did not know.. Slowly she narrated that how in past my father and Dubey uncle had decided that if my mother gave birth to a girl, she would be married to Manish to strengthen their bond of friendship between two families. Manish's mother had died when he was four years old and with the help of mother and Shukhiya chachi as maid Dubey uncle had reared Manish any how. That is why Manish was very much attached to my mother and us both. Now I knew that why my father and Dubey uncle seemed glad to see Gauri and Manish quarrel, humarously in childhood. I understood that why every year during brothers festival on Bhaiduj Manish was sent to his relatives at U.P. Mother further said that as per my father's wish and commitment, she wanted that both Manish and Gauri should be married soon in front of her eyes as she was not feeling well. Saying all this, mother looked exahsted. I and Gauri were listening very eagerly. I immediately understood the situation we were in. In all respect Manish was a good match for Gauri but I asked mother, had she asked about the praposal with Dubey uncle and Manish. Mother replied joyfully that she had done so and Dubey uncle had gladly gave his consent informing Manish as well. Mother further declared that she wanted to get this ceremony completed tomorrow itself. She further said that I should go to Pandit ji immediately and finalise the function. Hearing all this sudden devlopment of her marrige Gauri began to shade tears and immotionaly she said to mother, Maa I will do everything as per your wish but please get well soon, In our cast marriage function were done as per the consent of Pandit who seeing Planets condition declared the suitable date and time. When I approched Pandit ji and seeing both bride and grooms horoscope declared that next day is not proper for marriage but we could do finalising ceramony which was as proper as doing marriage itself. Mother agreed to that and inviting near relatives and friends next day evening in the presence of Pandit ji my little sister Gauri was vowed to Manish. Mother looked happy and full of energy, she did all the formalities rituvaly and blessed both Gauri and Manish embracing and praying God to shower happyness and prosperity to them. Sarrounded with us she felt proud and happy amidst photographed with us. Before going to bed at night she again called us and talked happily. She now looked tired so advised us to go and take rest. She slept peacefully but did not wake in the morning. All hell broke in the morning. We were weaping and blaming ourselves for not attending her properly. School staff and students in large numbar came to attend her funeral. With heavy heart I accomplished funeral duties. We both Gauri and me became dumb. One by one Father, Dubey uncle and now mother gone, we were left alone in this world. It was a shock for Manish also but he tried hard to console Gauri and me in everyway possible. On thirteenth day my immediate boss Mr. Vasudevan came to pay his homage and respect for the departed soal. He convinced me explaining Lord Krishna's Gita that the work of every person was predetermind by God's will and we should do our duties honestly without desiring results. He explained me my responsibilities of Gauri and advised me to join duties to forget the sadness. In between these days I saw vast changes in Gauri's behaviour. In stead of feeling aloofness, like me, she became more responsive than before. She kept her busy all day long doing all sorts of work which mother used to do. Before going back to join my duties it was decided that Gauri will complete her college education privately and will attend computer classes as usual, Manish will go to farm and in evening attend house needs. Sukhiya chachi as usual will look after everything conserning Gauri and Manish. I went back to join duties at oil rfinery. My fellow workers helped me a lot in forgetting my sadness by giving me more attention and respect. These uninvited thoughts, which came in my mind, exahsted me and ultimately I slept late in the morning.

CHAPTER 2

DOME

I heard a voice calling me and waking up, saw a girl standing at the door flap of tent and was calling Mr Amitabh Mr Amitabh please wake up please wake up. I immediately realised that I was not in Rampur but in Delhi exhibition ground. Hurriedly stud up, dressed and went forward to meet the visitor. A beautiful girl of my age, golden hairs, big eyes, shineing white teeth between red lips, wearing white swetar and black jeans extended her hand saying I am Tanya, Tanya Terishkova. When I took her hand she said in broken Hindi mere fadar ne apko pement dene ko bheja. She further said, vo bimar hain, apko bole, kya aap unse hatel men brekfast lenge, apko bulaya. I was astonished to hear a foreign girl speaking in Hindi language. I had never met a girl alone before and that too in Delhi. I was bewilderd and could not understand what I should do. I was still holding her hand. She hesitently withdrew her hand and taking out an envelope from the purse gave it to me. I took the envelope and said in hurry Miss Tanya you please wait here I am just comming. I took my backpack and ran towords utility house which was near by. Easing myslf, took a dry wash, got dressed, hairs combed and came back to the tent. When Tanya saw me coming she moved towords her car which was parked beside the road. I sat down in the front seat beside her and the car moved on. I had never been with a beautiful girl alone that too in a car. I was feeling awkward. A perfumed breeze was coming from all side. I began to talk unnecessarily about the weather, heavy traffic, rush of people etc. Time to time Tanya looked at me and smiled but said nothing. I wanted the drive to be continued for long but suddenly the car stopped. I saw that we have reached at Hotel Rajdoot and Tanya was waiting for me. I got down and followed her into the hotel. In a beautifuly decorated reception hall many guests and foreigners were busy talking and reading news papers. Following behind a tip top beautiful girl I was feeling that everybody was staring at us. Reaching second floor room no, two twenty two Tanya pushed the call batton. Immediately the door opened and Mr Terishkov welcomed me by shaking hands. Offering a seat he said that he was not feeling well and had some urgent call to attend so he had called his daughter from hostel to send the payment of work done last night. The room was decorated with big sofas, TV, flowers and coloured pictures on wall. Terishkov looked tired, not energetic as last day. He said to me now Mr Amitabh let us talk to business, before we could talk, the room service entered with a trolly full of snaks and drinks. Tanya came back from inside room and sitting beside her father served us breakfast. After taking omlette tost and two cups of coffee Terishkov looked better. He looked serious and said to me Mr Amitabh befor we talk bussiness tell me how come you were at the exhibition gate? I was not surprised. Slowly, I narrated about my work at Oriental fabricaters, how relieved for two months and to pass the time, looking for any suitable job was waiting at exhibition gate. At the same time the phone bell rang and

Terishkov began to talk in Russian. for four or five minutes. Tanya too was listening, the conversation and lookd worried. After talking Terishkov was silent for some time than diciding something he turned to me and said Mr Amitabh I have a praposal for you. My assistant who looked after all the work, is ill at Mumbai and is going back home to Russia tomarrow and I will have to do the pending work at the exhibition. You should understand that it will not be easy for me and with your experience and the work you did last night in time impressed me very much. Now taking out some coloured photographs, from the brief case he gave it to me and said please study these first than we will talk bussiness All pictures were that of a half moon type Dome taken in different stages and showed interior exhibited machines and other things. Three of the pictures attracted my attention. One of them showed a Dome with two rings and connected by chenals and penals. Second picture lookd Dome coverd, with a blue shining cloth and a board and flags in front. The same third picture was looking like a shining flying Saucer, a cap on Top. My mind was analysing all the details and I understood why Mr. Terishkov had calld me. When I looked back to him, he said can you assemble this Dome in fifteen days time. He further said that Ayangar and co. had a labour contract with him. His assistant a mechanical enginier, got it done in his supervision and after that worked as manager. He further said that as Ayangar and co. not responding and the assistant gotten ill, he was not sure how he will be able to manage all this in time. He said that he was ready to pay Rs. forty thousand for eraction of the Dome as was his contract with Ayangar and co. He further declared that if the work was done in time he was ready to offer me the post of Manager on Rs, twenty thousand for one month. Mr Terishkov was looking at me expectedly. Now it was my turn to think and reply. Looking to the experience I had gained working in the refinery, this was an easy job. Other details were not available. Only seeing photographs, it will be like doing by trail and error method, which will take more time. I was to ensure myself, whether I will be able to do it in given time of fifteen days. As per yesterdays experience I was sure that Mr Terishkov was in a jame and he needed help. Tanya too was looking at me anxiously with her father. I calculated in mind that for yesterday's work I had saved Rs six thousand which was a good sum and there was not any chance of getting job further. I thought that if I would be able to employ five to ten labours, the work could be done in time. Either way by payment wise or helping a needed person, it was a good proposal offered to me by Mr Terishkov. As the time was passing Mr Terishkov began to walk in the room uncomfortably. Tanya too seemed to be in tension. Deciding it with a sighe of relief I said to him Sir I myself will feel honourd to work under you and will do my best to finish the job you have favoured with me. Tanya ran to her father and embracing said something in Russian which I assumed was congratulation. All worries gone in a second Mr Terishkov lookd relieved he came to me, shook hand with me and sitting beside me said Mr Amitabh, you look to be a fine promising boy to me, now I am offering you a second proposal to you, would you like to work as manager of the exhibition from tenth Novembar to fourth decambar on payment of Rs twenty five thousand on work contract? I could not believe the words spoken to me. Previously I was in a mind to do any daily job which came in my way and the luck was giving me a prize of working as manager. I stud up and shaking hands with Mr Terishkov I said in Hindi that I will not disappoint him in any way. I dont think that he understood my words but he said Amitabh you look like a son to me and he will help me in all the way to promote my life in future. All tension gone we including Tanya took a second round of coffee. Mr Terishkov than typed a letter of work contract, another for my appointment as manager. With photographs he gave me the letters and advised me to live in the tent to facilitate the work smoothly. He than told Tanya to take me back to exhibition ground. Shaking hands with Mr Terishkov I took leave of him and came down in the reception hall. I could not understand what has happened to me. Either I had not slept last night well or the event just passed had excited me so much that I began to walk fast. Tanya literily, running behind me. Again I was talking aimlessly, confused but smiling Tanya accompnied me to the tent. When the car stopped at the tent I realised that Tanya opening the car door was waiting for me to come down. I felt ashamed and said I am sorry, Miss Tanyaa for talking aimlessly. Please forgive me. Smiling Tanya replied aap, subah se, difrent lage, achha lagaa, main hostal jati, fir milenge baay.

I looked at the watch and immediately rememberd that if I have to start the work from tomorrow I must start now. Going to the administrative office I gave them the authority letter and the application form to connect electrice and telephone connection. Completing the formalities I walked fast towards L&T site. The sairen was already sounding, when I reached there, workers were coming out for lunch and rest. I saw Jagdish and his friends coming out. I invited them for lunch at the cantene. Jagdish replied that they have their tiffin with them but I insisted saying we will share and enjoy both togather talking. They agreed. I, orderd eight tanduri chapati, two fried dal, two vegetable curry and salad. Talking and enjoying, I paid them Rs four hundred each for yesterdays work. Saying that the work was not worth that amount they took only three hundred each. Finishing the lunch, I said to Jagdish, Friends I am going to tell you the good news now. I have been given the chance of erecting a Dome at yesterdays sight and will require ten workers to help me. Jagdish tell me how you can help me in getting the workers. Immediately he exclaimed and said Pandit ji what for we are here. Our job at L&T is over now and within two days I will arrange more workers to join us. Gladly I announced that I will be giving Rs four hundred per day for ten days and if the need be, give them overtime also. We all shook hands and they promisd to come at nine o clock in the morning to do the work. Relieved that it is a good start I took an auto rikshaw and went to the room I had taken on rent. Paying the rent due I collected my belongings with drawing board and came back to the tent. On my way back I purchased some flexible wire, holder, pintop and bulb. Feeling tired I lied down on the bed and soon slept. A ringing bell woke me up and saw a telephone on the table. The line man answered sir you were fast sleep so I have connected the phone and the number is attached with it. Please dont mind. The electric line was also connected. Immediately I joined the flexible wire to the tent and the bulb began to glow. With the facility available to inform Mr Terishkov I phoned to Rajdoot hotel room, a female voice answered hello who speaking, I said Amitabh sharma from exhibition ground. Tanya began to speak in broken hindi, Oh main Tanya, fadar thik nahin, rest karte, kuchh kaam kya, I began to perspire, I had not talked with a girl before on phone. I immediately answered no no I phoned just to inform that electric and phone conection had been installed. Tanya said aap achhii Hindi bolte, main siikhti, meri frend juliyen, mujhe inglish sikhti, aap hindi men, baat kareng, to achchhaa. I said kripya fon numbar note kar lijiye, dictating the numbers I put down the phone immediately with a sighe of relief. Remembering that I have not talked with Gauri from last ten days I phoned her. The bell rang for some time but no answer. Now I began to blame myself for not taking proper care of my little sister who was alone at Rampur. I thought atleast if Gauri was not there sukhiya chachi should answer. But again thought she has become old and short of hearing, the door might be closed so again I phoned. After three rings Gauri answered sobbing Dadu you have become hardsouled. I have phoned many a time to your office but they only say, leave the massage that is all. I am too much worried. Tell me why it is so. I answered betu, I am going to tell you a good news. I have completed the job of refinary and am at Delhi now. My next job will start after two month. I was in two minds either I should go back to Rampur or try for a job here at Delhi. To try my luck I prefered trying here only. The good news is that I have got a good work here and after that I will be doing the job of manager in the exibition. Have you any news of Raju, Gauri immediately said yes bhaiya, hearing of mother he had come here and was very sad. Now adays, he has opened a travel agency and a flying club at Jaipur airport. He speaks English, very fluently, I have given him your address and number, your new number was not known to me but anyhow he will contact you in Delhi. I was pleased to know that Raju has come back to Jaipur. Then Gauri said bhaiya I have completed my computer course. Mr,Ayanger who used to teach us has gone back to chennai. Rathore uncle who had opened the computer cafe, pressed me a lot, to work in place of Mr.Ayanger, seeing my ability he had offered me a job of tuter in rupees four thousand a month. Without asking you I have joind as tuter. I have many friends now and I enjoy very much. Tell me if you are angry. I replied betu if you are happy then I am too. Tell me if you want anything from me, I will definately bring it with me when I come back. And where is Manish? In answer Gauri begain to complain that Manish talks unnecessarily and when I asked that do you quarrel with him, she replied, yes brother I do quarrel with him. As you know mother always liked our quarreling and so what mother liked, I will do forever. Gauri began to shout Mani-Mani there is a phone call for you from bhaiya. Manish answered immediately pranam bhaiya, I am well here, this year crop is very good. In the mean time grabing the phone again Gauri said bhaiya manish's maternal uncle had come for her daughters marraige with you. She is in service so I refused because I dont like service girls, I did the right thing or not? When I said that you too are serving then she replied that it is a temporary job and I am learning new things too. I said OK whatever you do and like is OK with me. I will talk to you after two days so take care and good bye. Now was the time for me to plan next days work. Generaly a sketch plan of numberd diferent stages is made to facilitate the assembling but at present it was not available so I had to make it first. I spread out the photographs on table and began to note the details. Measuring I observed that the width of the Dome was thrice in comparison than the height. Taking out a drawing sheet I drew a twelve c.m.line marking it as A and B. At the centre a four c.m perpendicular line marking it with C and D. with divider at point C I joined a curved line from point A to B. I made a small cap on point D. Then measuring the middle ring and the chanels shown in the photograph I drew those lines. Satisfied I compared it with the photographs of the Dome. They looked a like. I made up my mind that opening the big crates I will assemble the bottom ring first which will decide my further action of assembling. Pleased with my work of progress I went for a half an hour fast walk out side, washing did my routine prayaers. It was already eight in the night. I knew that from tomorrow I will not get enough time to relaxe and eat leisurly. Went to the canteen, finished my dinner at ease and went back to tent. With in five minutes I was fast sleep.

Biological clock woke me up at exactly on six. On backside wall tap, washed my mouth, drank two glass of water and relieved myself going to utility house. After doingYoga for half an hour in the tent, went out side and running took two rounds of the ground. Walking out side for a while to rest, took bath and sitting in front of table, where I have put up a picture of Tridev Gods Brmha, Vishnu and Mahesh prayed for a while. This was my routine taught by my mother who seriously worshiped daily in the morning. Some times I and Gauri also joined if woke up early. People say that if you do not worship to God He becomes angry but I thought differehtly. It was my assumption that God has created all creatures and human beings to do their prescribed work honestly and if they did it He is satisfied, otherwise He will judge and punish them accordingly as per rules. He would not mind whether you worship Him or not. Some times I too did not worship but I never repented. So after my prayers I dressed in working dress of Oriental Fabricater and went out to inspect the crates and make up my mind as to how to start from begining. I thought of Mr Vasudevan, my immediate boss at the refinery. Remembering his work of action, I searched for numbers and markings on the crates and boxes. I saw that they were numberd and in some with same numbers A, B, C, D was printed. It means they were part of the same group. Satisfied I drew a chair from the tent and sat down to wait for my assistants. It was alredy nine and the workers started coming in groups. I saw Jagdish with four companions, approching. I shook hands with them as Jagdish introduced. Jai and Omprakash I knew were experienced but Hari and Gopal were the new comers Jagdish had brought to help for misslinious work. I had to convince myself that in two three days they would be trained. Time of action has come and I was feeling at the height of energy. I sent Jai and Omptakash to bring breakfast of Pav and tea and to purchase coconut, flowers, sweets and other things to perform Puja for the blessing of God. Taking Jagdish and his friends with me I explained them to search for a box numbered one. After a while Hari found the box measuring six feet long wooden polished and sealed with cloth. It was heavy but we all managed to lift it and carry it in front of the tent. I saw a swastik made in front with red patches as if it has been worshiped many times. It was not unusual, workers always worship their Tools. By this time Jai and Omprakash had arrived. Chit chating we enjoyed our breakfast and washing our hands we opened the box. We became glad to see foam packd shining tools and seremoniously by tributing our respect, lighted scented stick. broke coconut and offerd sweets to God of Making Vishvakarma.

To begin, Jagdish and Jai started opening numbered two crate, which was the largest and screwd on top. Using bolt driver machine, in fifteen minutes they opened the top. On top of a thick plastic sheet they took out packed in a bag, a long rope with big nails attached on both ends and two in the middle and gave it to me. At first I was confused about the use of it but when I measured it I understood. It was made to make the round circle on which the outer and inner ring was to be assembeled. Gladly I explained them how to make a round circle. I have already decided that leaving enough space in front for flag poles and back for tent the Dome will be erected. By measuring the ground, one nail was fixed at the marked centre and tightening the rope Jagdish moving round at first scrached a circle in the middle with the help of pointed nail and after words a big outer circle. We congratulated Jagdish, the way he did it heaving labourously. When others were busy cleaning the ground I opened the tool box and surveyed inside, taking out ply covers. There were spaners, shovels, hammer and so many other tools which could be used in any job. Undernith were hundreds of colour markd bolts, all shining like new. On top a sylendrical machine with electric motor which looked like a lawn mower, attracted my attention. It had many ragged tooth on sylander. When I put it down on the ground and started the motor, it began to dig a trench on the ground. To understand the use of it I studied the photograph again, the bottom ring seemed to be below the ground level. It meant that we will have to use that machine at the outer and middle circle to make a trench where the beams will rest. The puzzle solved I became relaxed and calling Jai and Gopal I demonstrated them the use of that typical machine. Under supervision of Jagdish they started making a trench first in the middle and then outer side. I directed Hari to clean out the trench with shovel. At lunch time the first face of the work was completed. They had their tiffin with them but seeing the hard work they had done, I invited them to canteen for lunch and announcd that from tomarrow they will not bring tiffin with them but lunch with me at canteen, gladly they agreed.

After resting for half an hour Jagdish uncoverd the second plastic sheet, he saw long curved shining beam pieces. He took them out one by one. They were fifteen sixteen feet in length and five inches thick, about two inches raised in the middle with a rubber lined groove in it. In both outer and inner ends an eight inches circular ring, hole in middle, attached. It looked heavy but lifting it was so light, we were surprised. They were all numberd so starting from the front side we put them beside outer circle we have just prepared. Each piece had a groove in one side and a four inches extended chool to fit in the groove at other side. Measuring they began to dig and make room for the ring to fit in. Ring number two, five, eight and elevan had ten inches flat plate with holes in it were attached, a space was made for them also. After two hours labour they all helping together completed the job. The only thing remained was to fix all the beams togather one by one and put inside the trench we have made for them. Again I pressd them to rest for half an hour and take tea with me which Omprakash had brought from out side gumti. Fixing the beams togather was easy. The four inch chool was pressed in the other beam's groove and a slight jerk from the hammer joined them easily. At five o clock we have completed the job successfully. Shaking hands I congratulated them. I assured them that now on the work will be easier. They all went home chating and joking togather.. Feeling tired but full of acomplishment I lied down in the tent to rest and plan for tomorrow. I thought that to bear the load of Dome there must be a support from the center which could be removed afterwords and I will face the problem tomarrow.

Next day I told Jagdish to empty the big crate and keep them serialy on the ground. First were sixteen flat beam pieces, made of the same material, four of them had holes, in one side and ten inches round on the other side with holes. The other four were with ring on both sides. Remaining eight, were curved and had rings on both sides. Secondly Jagdish took out, twenty two, three feet long pointed foundation pyloons to jam the beam to the ground and after that nine round pipes were taken out. Eight of them were of the same size but nineth was bigger having two feet diameter plate on top side and holes in both sides. After this eight long pieces of curved beam with holes in end and upper side and seven small flat beams were taken out. Surveying all this I instructed them to put them in group serialy in ground. It was clear now that fixing the plates first, round pipes will be stood and above that middle ring will be fixed. Yesterday I had seen extra plates on four outer beams and the purpose of which I could not understand at that time. When both types of flat beam were joined togather, they came, upto the center.. When all four sets were put on beam two, five, eight and elevan they made a cross in centre having four rings on flat plates and bigger ring in the centre. The ramaining eight half curved beams with rings on both sides were put in the middle exacavated space, the puzzle solved itself. Trench was made for them and were tightend, with bolts. To fix the outer beam in place all the pointed foundation pyloons were pushed into the ground by hammering them. It was clear now that all nine round poles were to be fixed at the rings made by this way. When others were busy I took Omprakash with me to inspect crate number two which was unusual in size. It was screwed up by the side. When we opened it, we saw a big round drum with two feet plates around. When we two pulled, it came out easily. It had a door on one side below the plate and holes at the bottom. Above the plate, glass windows on all side. I understood that this is the cap I had seen in the photographs. Whoever had planed that Dome must be a genious I thought. Step by step I had to assemble as the markings direct to do. Jagdish and Omprakash looked happy at the work of progress. They too were astonished to see the workmanship and design of the dome. It was lunch time now so we all went to the canteen. Resting a while after lunch all the eight round pipes were fitted by bolts on the ring below. The nineth pipe was a bit different. It had a two feet diameter plate on top and a hinge at the bottom. It was heavy than others..At first we tightend the hinge than lifting it from other side gradualy it stud up and was screwed to the bottom ring which was larger than others. When they were busy tightening the round poles, I was examining other boxes when I saw Tanya coming towords the tent in car. My heart began to run faster thinking how I will talk to her in front of others. I immdiately ran forward to the car. Stoping the car and getting down Tanya said smiling, khush khabar laaii, aap baithne ko nahin bolenge, I immediately replied oh Tanya not here please, come with me to canteen. Riding with her on car, we reached canteen. It was empty at this time. We sat down on a corner seat and I orderd coffee. So near and alone for the first time I watched her minutely. She was very beautifull. For the first time when I had seen her in front of tent she resembled a face I admired much but now sitting in front of me I was looking at my twentieth centuries favurate heroin Madhuri Dixit's replica, same bobd cut cloudy hairs upto shoulders, the same smiling eyes, shining beautifull teeth between rosy lips. The only difference was in the way of talking as she was Russian. I continued to stare her and by feeling the heat of my staring, her cheeks became redder, her head lowered a little she began to search something in her purse. The time had stopped, no sound was coming to me, I only could see was that a beautifull girl was sitting near me, a nostalgic fragerance ingulfing me. Suddenly Tanya lifted her head and smiling spoke in hindi kal fadar bole, aaj lai, russiyan men likha, padh kar sunati. Suddenly I came to senses I felt as if I had fallen from the sky to the ground. My face became red in shame. For the first time in life I understud what it means to be near a beautifull girl. I became annoyed with me. I was relieved when the waiter put coffee infront of us. I said hurriedly please Tanya tell me what is written in the paper. Tanya smiled and began to read first in russian than translating it in hindi. sab boks men nambar likha, ek ek nikalo, rang dekhna, takat nahin lagna, nahin thokna, khud fit hoga, dekoreshan kagaj skech buk kes men hay, kathin ho fon se puchho, gudlak. Tanya was saying all this slowly and in between she looked at my face. She began to understand that nothing is clear and she became to look worried. An unknown girl in a foreign country, finding her father in distress was trying to help us both in any way possible. Sympathising with her I immediately took her both hands in mlne and said smiling, oh Tanya realy this is a great help to me and now I know what is to be done. Please rest assured and thanks for your help. Tell dady that he should not worry any more now. I will complete the work in time. Tanya half believing me tried to smile but said aap thiik bolte na, der hoti, jana padega, dedy ko batana, fir yunivarsity jana, ab main jaatii. Leaving me at the tent, saying goodby Tanya went back. I sighed in relief and pleasure of meeting her. By the time I returned from the canteen Jagdish and his friends had tightened all the eight round pipes on bottom rings. I took them all to the drum shaped observation post which looked heavy but when we lifted it, were surprised for its its lightness. Effortlessly we brought it to the centre. It was to be fitted on top of the nineth pole at centre. I inspected it minutely. It had a door with a round wheel at the place of lock and when I pushed it anti clock wise, the door opened. It was an observation post having glass windows covered with strong mash. At the top there too I could see a wheel and when I moved it a round door opened out side, climbing on a chair fixed at the base, I could see the sky. There were hooks on each four side and two hand grill beside outer door. In between on both side of the door a set of holes to screw some thing. I was puzzeled to think its use in an exhibition. It had a two feet round plate with holes underneeth. The big round pole also had a round plate on top with holes. Matching the colours marked in them Jagdish tightened them with bolts togather. Omprakash and co. looked worried as to how it can be lifted without any mishap. First I instructed them to lift the observation post a little so that poles bottom which had a hinge could be tightened to the center ring. This done I told them to lift it from the posts side gradualy pushing upwords and move towords centre. It stud up easily on the center and was tightened by four bolts of the hinges. Hari and Gopal looked amagingly open mouthed. I congratulated Jagdish, Jai and Omprakash, Hari and Gopal. smiling. The siren announcing the time to go I invited them for tea at the gumti outside before they went home. I was satisfied with the progress we have made. I had a clear vision of how it will be completed in time. Only one question came into my mind again and again was, this Dome was not designed for exhibition purpose, it meant for another but for what? I consoled myself thinking I was there to do a job and should not think otherwise.

It was the third day When Jagdish opened the third big crate. He took out eight slight side curved thick beams with one end groove and other end chools like bottom beam with holes on middle. In lower side two holes in middle. Another eight beams had holes in centre and many groovs in distance. Benith them were two small and one big ladder and bundels of rope and packed in cartoon six pairs of shoes, hornesses and steal accesseries were taken out. I immediately understud that today I had to be carefull as only Jagdish, Omprakash and Jai were the experienced worker, other two Hari and Gopal were new. Standing on ladders and tightening bolts was a tricky job in fixing the middle beam. I had observed that all the eight round poles had angled plates on top with one hole on each side. It means that two persons on seprate ladder will hoist the beam to poles height and third person at centre will tighten the beam with bolts. I got them assemble two beams froov and chool pushing and slight hammering, trained them to hoist two beam asscending on ladder and when they approved the method, the final work began. Hari and Gopal holding the side ladders and myself at centre ladder, Jai and Omprakash at each end lifted the numberd beam, asscending the ladder, put the beam on first round pole's plateand than on second poles plate, Jagdish standing at the center ladder supported the beam and tightened it with two bolts each. The tricky part started now. The third beam has to be uplifted first, putting it on the third pole and pushing hammering it to join in second beam was a bit difficult but Jagdish on cener ladder did it and screw it to the third pole. Slowly beam number four, five were fixed and tightened. Now six, seven and the first beam was to be joined. It was the most dificult. First we joined beam and six togather at ground and hoisted them togather omprakash's ladder at number five beams end and Jai's ladder at first beam biganing, Jagdish on center ladder pushed down heavyly and with a jerk both beam five and six came down on plates of pole six and seven. Beaming with pleasure Jagdish tightened them with screws. I began to clap loudly and congratulated them for their pains and effort. I knew this beam was the base for fixing chenal and penal. Another top eight beams were to be fixed when the chenal and penal would be in place. The Dome started taking shape. After lunch and rest, crate nomber four was opened and two types of four inch thick chenals were taken out. Half of them were long and rest short in length having holes on three sides. Like middle beam these chenals too were, in two parts. First the base chenal, above them penals and on the top final chenal will be fixed. Everything was so well designed that you will have to do them accordingly otherwise they will not fit. Special grooves were made on the foundation beam for chenal and penal. All the chenals were put on the ground matching the number than Omprakash and Jai took one plain end and taking hold pushed it into the beam. Jagdish took the other end with holes, asscended the big ladder, put it on the middle beam above and tightened it with bolts. Hari and Gopal were to hold the ladder and move it to another place as directed by Jagdish. The same procedure has to be followed again and again. This way all the bottom chenals were fixed except the last one, where the exhibition gate will be. After taking tea I explained them, how the other half upper chenals will be fixed. It was to be done just the opposite way. Now Omprakash and Jai had to sit on the plate of observation post and to push the chenal into the plate while Jagdish on middle beam will tighten it with bolts. Hari will hold the ladder and Gopal will send the chenal to Jai above by tightening it with rope hanged for this purpose. These chenals were half in length and light wait Wearing harness Omprakash and Jai reached at the top plate by asscending two ladders we have joined to rest at the top. The process of fixing top chenal's started again, first slowly than faster and by the time five, all chenals in place looked like the Dome in shape. Sitting on chairs and boxes in front of the tent, we all looked happy. To celibrate we had tea once more and cheered.

This was the forth day and the pressure of unknowm obsticals removed I was at ease now doing my all daily rituals, feeling relaxed was about to go out side of the tent when I saw Tanya entering the tent. She was laughing and embracing me, held my hand and took me out of the tent. I was bewilderd when I saw Mr. Terishkov, standing beside the car smiling. I was not expecting him at this time but went forward and wished him good morning. He shook my hands and said, well done my boy, how could you have done this much of the work without any help from any body. I am proud of you. He looked better. I said to him, no sir, dont thank me, thanks to the engners who made this wonderful Dome in such a way that I could assemble it without any dificulty. I will thank Tanya too to give me proper guidence in time and necessary papers of the Dome. Now Tanya began to say Amit ji, papa chintit the, bimar ho gaya, ab sab thiik hoga, aapko dhanbad. By this time Jagdish and his friends had come and were looking at us from a distance. I calld them and introduced them to Terishkov. He congratulated them for my assistance and saying good by returned to the hotel. I was glad that Mr Terishkov had recovered from the guilt he was feeling for his inability in performing the erection of Dome in absence of his assistant.. Anybody facing this situation will feel the same. Relaxed I phoned Gauri. I knew that she will be annoyed for not phoning her in last four days. She immediately began to sob, saying Manish had brought the two cows and calfs at home and she had to attend them, cleaning the cowshade, bathing and milking them. She further said Sukhiya chachi was too glad in bringing the cows at home. She worshipd them and gave them variety of foods to eat. When I asked her about Raju she replied in affirmative saying he will call me soon. When I asked why did not she had calld me before, knowing my phone number she lookd embraced and replied, she was so busy and could not get time. I said Gauri you already know that I am very busy in the new work so phone me whenever you like. I put down the phone and was glad that she had enough work to bussy herself. As usual this was the time for my daily round of running so completing it, did my prayers and coming from canteen relaxed, slept soundly.

Fifth days work started as usual opening the fifth big crate. As expected it contained shining one inch thick penals. They were big in size, arond six feet wide at bottom with two raised two inch block, four inch above from the bottom while upper side penal was around four feet wide having many holes. They lookd heavy but light in wait. Putting the harness and safty hook Omprakash and Jai asscending the ladder hooked themselves to middle beam.

Hari and Gopal lifted the first panel and keeping that on the lining groove of the bottom beam, with plastic hammer when they hit the two inch block, the penal went inside the lined groove. The penal was now resting on the two chenals already fixed previous day. Omprakash and Jai taking turn gradualy tightened the penal on middle beam with bolts. Under the supervision of Jagdish one by one all penals were in place before the siren sounded at five o clock evening. Passers by looked, in amagement, as to how, only five men were doing the heavy work easily. When I lied down on the bed inside the tent to rest I began to think an easy way to fix the above penals because the lower side of the middle beam was blocked by penals undernith and from inside bolting them, would be dificult. Finding no proper answer I again took out the photographs and began to study them minutely. In one of them, there were no poles in center in stead machines and other goods were displayed. It means the poles were removed and that too many a times. I began to calculate and came to the conclusion thar bottom and middle beam with chenals and penals tightened will bear the load of full structure effectivly. The problem I was going to face was the decoration and placement of machinery of which I had no experience. I was busy thinking all this when the phone started ringing. The heart gave a sudden beap and when I lifted the phone the voice said Dadu, neither it was Gauri's nor Manish's voice, than who could be that person calling me Dadu and suddenly rememberd it was Raju, my beloved old friend. I began to shout, oh Raju where have you been all these days, I had been waiting for you since long. No news of you from any where. When Gauri told me that you have come back and are at Jaipur I am dying to meet you. Raju laughingly replied, I will tell you everything my dear friend. I am reaching Delhi tomarrow morning at ten and will stay whole day with you. I will satisfy all your complaints. I myself had to talk with you everything of me, you and others. Hoping a great day tomarrow and how early the morning comes I went to sleep.

Waking early in the morning, I went to the utility room and completing toilet and bath, did yoga and prayers with joy and dressing up went to the exhibition gate. I informed the gate security about Rajkumar chauhan's arrival and came back. Three fourth of the work was completed and so at nine o clock when Jagdish and his co workers came, they were in a jolly mood even Hari and Gopal were more active. Without my telling them they took out the upper penals which were half in length comparing to lower penals from the crate and put them inside the Dome ground. They were busy in doing their work but I was anxously waiting for Raju. Suddenly I saw a black shining jeep coming towords the tent, sounding horn Raju arrived. I saw a wll dressed man with big mustachs getting down from the jeep. He was none other than Raju. We both ran towords each other and embraced, engulfing with both arms. We both were speechless only caressing behind. Holding his hand I took him inside the tent and made him sit in front of me. Tears of happyness in our eyes we two looked at each other for some time. As always he was well dressed, had gained weight and the mustache has increased his personality. Than Raju taking hold of my hands asked me about my mother's untimely death. He too had lost his mother in childhood and whenever he came to my house, mother always gave him love and affection like a son. I told him everything from the begining. When I told him about the engagement of Gauri with Manish, He became glad and said this is the best thing ever happened. He further said that it looks as if they were made for each other, though they quarrel some times but care for each other since childhood. Raju praised Gauri saying she had asked him to bring books on stars, planets and astroids. He was glad for her intrest on other things but some times between talks, he had seen her stareing in the sky searching for something he could not understand. When I enquired about him, he began to say, Dadu you and Manish had gone to college so I was left alone. To fullfill my dream of treking and mountaniering, I first went to Dehradun and afterwords to Darjling to learn mountaniering. I have now opened a travel agency and flying club at Jaipur airport. I am always busy taking foreign tourist, travling around Rajasthan and hill station. When I asked Raju, why he had not married so for, he replied sighing, he had met many girls but they were not of his liking. He wanted a dashing girl whose liking resembels his liking. In the mean time Jagdish enterd the tent and informed me that they had taken out all the penals from the crate and are waiting for my further instruction. I introduced him to Raju and we all went inside the Dome. When Raju looked at the rope, harnesses and steel hookes, he asked me about their use here. I replied that I did not know what for they are there. He became glad and said Amitda they are used for climbing the ridges where no foot holds exits. Tell me if any job is pending still. I now explained him about the fixing of chenals and penals to the top. He began to laugh and puting on a harness selecting a jamer he fixed it in a rope hanging from the top and using the jamer reached to the top easily. Jagdish and his friends were watching this facinated. Raju got down by the rope and said dont worry, he will trained them in few minutes. He made them wear harness and trained them one by one. I tried myself and praised my luck for the coming of Raju at the right time. The problem of staying on top and middle beam, safely attached with harness Hari and Gopal on top plate and Jai and Omprakssh at middle beam they pulled chenals by rope and keeping it in place tightened them with bolts as they had done earlier at bottom. By lunch time all the chenls were fitted and we all went to the canteen for lunch. Resting a while Raju went to the garage for servicing of the jeep and we became busy in fixing the upper penals. After that hanging with rope and supported by harness the upper chenals having holes in both sides were tightened with bolts. By shaking and hammering we again checked each and every chenal and penal. Assembling of the Dome completed we all serveyed it proudly and had tea togather. I congratulated them once more and to celibrate I offerd them next days leave before we start the decoration work inside. When Jagdish and his colligues went home rejoicing I too went inside the tent to rest. Though I had not done any work manualy but the load of responsibility had tired me. Fully relaxed, now I made up my mind to spend next day with Raju in sight seeing. Thinking all previous days work and problems I went to sleep and suddenly woke up when some body shook me saying Amitabh, Amitabh. I saw Mr Terishkov inside the tent smiling. I stud up immediately appolising. Tanya was standing at the door. She too was smiling and looked happy. Coming out of the tent Mr Terishkov shaking hands said once again I have to thank you, you have done it in a record time, that is inimaginable. I think you need a rest now for atleast one day and celibrate. I thanked him and replied sir I have already given next days leave to my workers. My friend Raju has come and we two are going to sight seeing tomarrow. Mr Terishkov immediately began to say, son if you dont mind, do me a favour. Take Tanya with you, at least she will see some good sights in Delhi as I am not familiyar with all of them. Hiding my pleasure of being with Tanya for a full day I replied immediately sir, I will be too pleased to give company to miss Tanya. From the corner of the eyes I saw Tanya smiling with pleasure. He further said afterword I would like that you have dinner with us. If your friend comes, bring him also. Beaming with pleasure I said thanks for the dinner sir, I will be too pleasd to come. I went to the car with them and said goodby. When they had gone I lied down again on the bed waiting for Raju who came back at eight o clock. We dined togather at canteen and after that, lying on the bed talked and remeberd our happy childhood days till midnight. I told him the news how Mr Terishkov my boss had asked me to take her daughter Tanya with us for sight seeing next day.

Next day morning after taking our breakfast at gumti outside, sitting on chairs, in front of tent we began to wait for Tanya to come.We saw two girls wearing salvar suit, walking on other side of footpath. They went ahead than came back and were waiting on footpath looking towords us.. The front tanned bold looking girl was saying something to the girl behind. Suddenly Raju stud up and hailed the girl in front saying madam are you both seem to be looking for some one? May I help you? Confused I said to Raju, what are you doing, you will get me insulted if nothing else. By this time the bold loking girl had come near to us and said yes, yes I am looking for Mr. sharma, Amitabh sharma. I became bewilderd as I did not know any girl in Delhi, before I could say anything Raju began to say, madam, you have come to the right place. This here gentle man is Amitabh sharma. Hearing this the girl extended her hand towords me and said Mr sharma I am your friends friend Juliyen, dont you recognize me? I took her hand in mine with surprise but could not reply immediately. I do understud that she is not Indian but a foriegn girl. The dilact seemed to be American. In a sweet voice she said, I am Juliyen, Don't you remember me? Still I was holding her hand and she was smilling mischiviously. She said again you seemed to be disoriented Mr.sharma. I am your friend's friend. Now let me introduce you, by other hand she pulled the girl standing behind, in front and said meet my friend, miss Tanya Teriskova. Tanya's face had become red and with Juliyen they both were gigling. Imbraced as I was, leaving Julien's hand I graped Tanya's hand and began to laugh. Untill now Raju was looking all these acts very eagerly. To overcome my shame I said welcome both of you. Now let me introduce you to my childhood friend. Raju immedeatly understood that this act has been done by Julyen, so he gave his visting card to Juliyen shaking hands with her and began to say, yes young lady I am Rajkumar chauhan, your friend's friend's friend. You may call me Raju. I knew that you were coming but you took too much of a time reaching me. Me and my fliying queen are waiting for you since morning. Now it was Julyen's turn in imbracement. She had not excpected this type of responce. Seeing me and Tanya laughfing Julien too began to laugh. Tanya began to say in Hindi ye dress ham pahle pahne hain. Juliyen fon ko manaa kiya, sarpraij dene ko. aap bura nahin manenge. Ab ghumne chalen. Raju immediately replied miss Tanya you two are looking beautiful in Indian dress and were sucessfull in surprising us. You both just wait here. I am coming in a jiffy. He came back in seconds with Jonga jeep sounding horn and stopped it in our front jerkly.

In front plate, written FLYING QUEEN, two search lights in front bar, sofa seats in the back, shining in morning light, the jeep looked beautifull. Getting down, Raju once again bowd to them saying Raju at your service madam. Seeing this beautifull jeep, both Juliyen and Tanya looked impressd. Juliyen asked Is this yours Mr Raju? Raju replied, It was madam now we both are hooked and booked to you my lady. Tanya and I began to laugh but Juliyen's face became red in shame. Raju further said you all come along in the front because back seat is already ingaged. We saw a Guitar and two bags there. We all four, Raju at the driving seat, than Juliyen, Tanya and I at the corner, sat down. Instantly the jeep started moving slowly up to the gate and after that it began to speed up like flying in the air as written on front plate. The sweet musice coming from the stereo and rush of air began to exhiliate us. The distance of ten km. to Kutub Minar he covered in ten minutes. Tanya and Juliyen shriekd when Raju avoided two acsidents. We took deep breath of relief when the jeep stopped at Kutub Minar. Raju was at his full form of enjoyment. Pulling us by hand he took us to the garden and started a variety of games, we enjoyed racing and joking teasing each other. His movie cemra in hand and on stand, took single and group phptographs. Running we went to the top of Kutum Minar was a thrilling experience. Tiring a little, sitting beside fountain he began to sing a song, aaja re aaja re mere dilvar aaja, dik ki pyas bujha ja re. with guitar. We applaud requesting him to continue. He said miss Juliyen this song is for your honour and sang, bhool gaya sab kuchh, yad nahin ab kuchh, bas itni si yad hai baki, juli I love you, I love you. Hearing her name and understanding the meaning a little Juliyen turned red avoiding Raju's stare. Tanya and Juliyen both were mesmriged and congratulated Raju for his voice and the way he was singing. We felt as if our child hood days were back again. I understud as to why Raju's travel agency was popular. Exhasted as we were and feeling hungry Raju advised us to go for a lunch some where on highway. From Mehrauly Raju took us to Raja Dhaba eight km. away. The sardar owner seated us beneath a tree in two wooden beds. Raju orderd, variety of dishes, tanduri, parathe, two vegitable curry, fried dal all with butter. Tanya and Juliyen were not acustumed in eating by hand so Raju taught them the way by giving example. Slowly they too begin to enjoy the food. When we finished our lunch Tanya said khana bahot achcha, hastal men khana bor hote. Hearing this Raju asked well Miss Tanya, how in hostel, dont you live with you father? Tanya said apko amitji ne nai bataya kya. Raju said now young lady, we spent such a marvelous time togather and had lunch but it seems we know very little about each other. Let us first introduce ourselves to strengthen our friendship. We all were looking at Raju expectedly. Finding a rich, jolly, handsome young person between them Tanya and Juliyen were impressd and eagerly wanted to know him much more. Raju began to say as Amit knows my mother and father died early leaving a fortune for me. My uncle brought me up. I spent my childhood with Amit as my best friend. After high school I went to Dehradun and Darjling and Kathmandu to learn treking, mountainiaring and flying. As per my liking I have opened a Travel agency near Jaipur Airodrum. I travel all over India taking small groups of foreigners. You are fortunate that you have a family. I have everything but am all alone in this world except Amit to think and care about me. Remembering my childhood days I am still alive. I am wandering alone in this world, Living this type of living is no living. In all four years, the time I have spent with all of you, are the most memorable moments of my life. Saying all this imotionnaly Raju became silent. Hearing the past story of Raju, Tanya and Juliyen were watching Raju, in amagement, they could not believe that this young handsome and jolly person could be so sad in life. Taking a deep breath Juliyen began to say about herself in broken Hindi and in english. Ther is nothing more about me. fadar amerikan, madar mexikan, car axident men dono died. main ten years ki thi, panch sal faster hom men rahi, passed high school, started working, part time kiya, aur nursing sikhi. Worked at hospital. I love swimming so joined at Miami beach, as safty guard. saved some money, took admission in university. Under youth exchange program, got scholarship and I am here at Delhi University. I have no relatives that I know. My room mate Tanya is the only friend I have in the whole world. The sad story of Juliyen had sarrowed the atmosphere. Tanya started saying mery madar jerman, fadar rashiyan. sukhi family, ham tomask men rahte. grand fadar ko gaurment diya, bahot thand hota. lisa bahan madar sath rahti. fadar is sal ritayer honge. maine to padhke sarvis karne ka hai, kaise hoga nahin samjhti. In my turn, I narrated from the begining. Mother and father's death, service at oriental and how at the gate of exhibition ground Mr Terishkov helped me by giving a chance to assemble the Dome. It seemed that we all were traveling in the same boat of fate, searching the unknown future. Suddenly Raju stud up, and putting his hand on the center of the table, said, friends as we know each other now, let us join our hands togather and take a vow that in future, to fasten our new friendship, we will be in contact with each other and help in any way possible. One by one Juliyen,

Tanya and myself put our hands on top of Raju's hand, closed our eyes and prayed God the almighty for few seconds. Opening our eyes we all were smiling and congratulating each other for new born unbreakable friendship. Raju driving slowly now, we all returned to the tent singing a song bachpan ke din bhula na dena, Tanya and Juliyen looked happy and joined singing as well as they could sing. We stopped at the exhibition gate where Tanya had parked her car. Tanya shaking hands with Raju thanked him for giving them good time and asked to come for dinner at night. Raju promptly replied if Juliyen was coming he would come certanly. On this comment we all began to laugh. Juliyen too enjoyed the comment and with a promise to meet at eight in the night, saying goodby, they both went back to hotel.

Coming in the tent to rest and pass the time, we both lied down on the bed fully relaxed and soon went to sleep. At about seven when I tried to wake Raju waking up he complained about disturbing him in a good dream. Both of us, feeling excitement at hand, washed, dressed hurriedly and reached the hotel room at eight thirty sharp. When I knocked at the door it opened immediately and Tanya welcomed us. Mr Terishkov shook hands with us saying, no introduction please, I know Mr Amitabh and this here gentleman must be Rajkumar, the girls were highly talking about. They had described each event like fairy tales, I am thankfull to both of you for giving those poor girls, good time, and what a nice pair of good friends you both are, surpassing each other in different qualities. Now please come along with me. The dinner table was set but beside the table Tanya was decorating candles around a Birthday cake. Raju looked at me enquiringly which I denied because I myself did not know about it. Mr Terishkov turned towords us and said this here dinner was overdue for Mr Amitabh as he had done a tremendous job in making exhibition Dome in record time, but to avoid formalities I had not informed you earlier, was that today is the twenty fourth birthday of Tanya's only best friend Juliyen. We both congratulated Juliyen. And she standing between them smiling with pleasure cut the cake and we all sang the birthday song many a times wishing Juliyen a happy long life. Mr Terishkov, then cutting small pieces of cake sweetend our mouth. After that Tanya served customery drink in small glasses and we tosted them for long happy life of Juliyen. We all enjoyed our dinner talking and telling previous small incidents enjoying. At about ten thanking for the dinner and saying good night we returned back.

Raju, lying on the bed began to say Amit this was his luckiest day of life. Meeting Juliyen he felt as if he had found his dream girl and the wayTanya was looking at me he thinks that Tanya loved me. He further said that he was going to prapose Juliyen for marriage. I immediately objected his saying and said Raju it was true that I liked Tanya very much but how could he say like that when in the morning itself had made a vow to be friends forever and help each other in future. You very well know that after exams will be over, she will go back to America and what will happen afterwards, nobody knows. It will be a great thing if we continued to be friends when they went back to their country. Raju stud up and said Amit, you are wright, we should not think about it in this way. We should wait for some time and than decide. He further informed me that he had an appointment with an American family next day morning so embracing me with a promise that he will come soon Raju was gone. Left alone thinking for next days work I too went to sleep.

Next day morning I surveyed inside the Dome and came into the conclusion that only three jobs were left to be done. First was to remove all the centre poles so that all the exhibits material could be displayed properly, second was to fix the fron gate and the last would be decoration and dislpay. I rememberd about the paper which Tanye had read informing that I had to proceed the work, step by step taking out all the material serialy and fix them looking to colours marked in them. At that time I had not given any importance to that suggetion but unknowingly I had done that in the same way. I felt sorry for that misunderstanding. I was sure now that this Dome was made for some other purpose and is being utilised for touring exhibition. Any how I would be pleased to complete it in time as promisd. By the time Jagdish and his companians arrived, I had finaly decided as to how effeciantely the poles would be removed. The middle beam and chenals fitted with penals would easily bear the load of struchure. Two at a time Jagdish and Omprakash standing on the ladder, unscrewed the bolts of top plate and then removing the bolts from the bottom ring, slowly pushed the pole side ways and the pole came out easily. They became glad and in an hour all the poles were removed and taken to their box. Now I was facing the problem of removing the center pole which was fixed at the bottom plate of observaion post. I imagined that if the post above was to be used again and again, it must be conected with the ladder so when I inspected the longest ladder I saw a plate with holes in either side and the same holes were in the post above on either side, I had seen previously. The puzzle clicked. I explained Jagdish the procedure. They put the big ladder beneeth the post holding firmly and jagdish bolted the ladder to the post. To remove the center pole we did the opposite. At first Jagdish unscrewed the plate bolts of the post undernith and then unscrewed the ladder bolts he had tightened earlier with the post. Now was the time to remove the big round center pole of the Dome who was bearing the full load of struchure. Hari, Gopal and Jai were in doubt whether the Dome would be intact or fall down. I explained them about the arches, we make in house building. Satisfied, Jagdish at first removed the two bolts of bottom hinges and all five pushing the pole opposit side, gradualy put it down on the ground. The ease with which it all was done, they looked surprised and hence, clapped loudly shaking hands togather. I congratulated them for their efforts and asked them to rest a while before going to lunch. Fixing the main colepsible gate in the front was easy. The upper chenals and penals above the center beam had already been fixed earlier so two portions of gate we fixed on the chanel number one and elevan, with the steel chenal in top and bottom provided for this. Along with gate, twelve coloured flag poles of twenty feet, one pole of twelve feet with Russian flag, plus two sets of chained three feet long poles were taken out. All these were fixed in front of the gate towords road. Out side work completed, the box with a book mark was brought in. The box contained one big album on which details of every table, raxe and the way they to be installed were shown serialy. Inside were thousands of leaflets packed in seprate bags, big coloured curtains and two sets of dresses. From crate seven bundles of flooring and two wheel barrows were taken out. Cleaning and leveling the ground the carpet was spread out on the ground. Crate eight and nine contained set of colourd plyboards for display tables. Starting from the gate, as shown in the album, all display tables were assembled. A small coverd cabin with glass door too was made in the back. With the help of wheel barows all left over boxes were put against their numbered display tables. The whole set up was beautifuly designed. One had to enter from the gate and moving slowly surveying all the displayed material would go outside of the Dome. When all were busy Mr Terishkov came in. I was surprised to see him, I introduced him to my fellow workers. He shook hands with them and praised for their labour. When I asked him about large curtains, he immediately directed Jagdish and Omprakash to fix the curtains in the hooks below center beam on chenal one and three. and below on the foundation beam. Like wise all the curtains were hanged and jeep fastened togather. A beautifull round display hall was ready, only thing left was the materials to be displayed on the tables and electrification. Mr Terishkov informed us that he will come in the morning and will get them installed as they need some expertise. I was feeling as if I had completed a long race against time and had won. Before going to canteen I did my prayers with gratitude and humbleness which God had bestowed upon me.

Ninth day morning all boxes containing display material were brought inside and under Yuri Terishkov's direction all the items were put on the tables. The variety of goods surprised us. They covered all aspects of life. Latest inovation of everything we could think of. By five o clock in the evening inside job was finished. Tennth day morning Jagdish and Omprakash opened a big box which contained a tent and its furnishing bed, table, chairs etc. and was made ready near the back wall. Another box contained electric fixtures and wiring. With in two hours a huge bell shaped LED pendent at the bottom of ex. post and round tubelights on the middile beam were fixed and connected to the switch board at the cabin. In the cabin itself a big screen TV, computer and office table, chairs and air conditioning was done. After lunch, out side light decoration of the Dome started. The top observation post and all the chenals, from top to bottom, were decorated with moving coloured LED bulbs. Jagdish and his friends were in a great spirit, working lights were on, tirelessly working, when we finished it was already dark. Tanya and Juliyen too had arrived. We all assembled in front of the Dome to look the result of our labour and celibrate. Mr Terishkov invited all in front of the cabin inside. He lighted candles and smelling sticks and prayed for some time and than asked Tanya to switch on the main switch. The result was astonishing. We were amidst milky lights coming from all sides. We all clapped cheering aloud. Terishkov shaking hands with Jagdish and his partner, congratulated them heartly and distributed sweets, which Tanya had brought. Outside in moving lights, the Dome looked as if a Flying Saucer had landed there. We congratulated each other and I paid them each Rs. four thousand for ten days working, plus one thousand as bonus. They looked happy, I tookdown the address and mobile no. of Jagdish and Omprakash so that they could be called for dismantelling in time. When I came back in the cabin Yuri Terishkov, Tanya and Juliyen again congratulated me again. I replied that thanks should be given to those enginers who had made this wonderful Dome. I had only assembled it as per their instructions. Yuri terishkov looking at me praiseingly said now Amitabh as promised earlier from tomaorrow you are going to take the charge of Manager of this exhibition, next day at three p.m there is an interview for six demonstration girls, previously it was done by Dimitriz my assistant, I have no experiance for that, so what is your suggestion? Stammering I replied sir, I too have no experiance and that too to girls, I myself will be nervous. Tanya and Juliyen began to laugh hilariously. Looking to our problem Juliyen said uncle, if you dont mind, I will interview the girls, you just watch and from my signal, if you are satisfied with the candidate, select her. It is that simple. We both sighed in relief. Yuri Terishkov said, yes my sweat daughter, you are as bright in mind, as well as in beauty. All happy with the suggestion we enjoyed coffee and pastries Tanya had brought and they departed saying goodby, to meet next day at two pm for interview. Resting a while, taking bath again I did my prayers sitting in front of Tridev God Bramha, Vishnu and Mahesh with sanskrit shloks and lighted smelling sticks. I humbly thanked them again and again for giving me courage to face the problems time to time and completeing the job without any mishap. Returrning back from the canteen I wanted to share the happyness I phoned to Gauri. Manish answered saying Dadu Pranam, everything here is well Gauri must be coming after doing her daily worshipping. I asked again does Gauri still quarels with you. Manish answered no Dadu sometimes she does and I feel happy for her doing teasing. Now Dadu tell me whether you too worship there without any temple with you. I replied Manish it is not necessary to have a temple with you, by simply The Gods picture in front and praying with devotion you feel peace and strength in mind but why are you asking this? Manish replied Dadu, like mother Gauri is busy morning and evening worshpping and celbrates all holy functions seriously. Sometimes I saw her looking at the sky searching. One day I heard her speaking if she would have a telescope it will be better. I do not kanow why. When Raju came she had asked him to bring some books from Jaipur library. She is busy all the time. Gauri has come, talk to her. I asked Gauri if she was well there and said I have to give you a good news that I have finished my work contract in time and have saved much more money than expected and from tomarrow I would be working here as Manager. In alternet days I will talk to you. Tell me if you want anything I will send it through Raju. Gauri said Brother you have told me a very good news but tell me one thing, who are Tanya and Juliyen Raju bhaiyaa was talking about. He was telling that they both are your friends but you never told me about them. You seem to be hiding things from me also. I immediately replied Gauri you know that since Raju became a guide, he talks too much. Tanya is my Boss's daughter and you know very well that my boss is Russian. Juliyen is her American room mate. I introduced them to Raju and he is now talking big things about me. Gauri immediately said Bhaiya please introduce them to me, I would like it very much. I will impress my friends telling about them. Tell me would you do that please. I satisfied her by telling that with in two or three days I will fullfill her desire. Than when I asked her about the telescope she looked shocked and began shouting Manish Manish and said Bhaiya I dont know what he complains about me to you but buy me a cheap telescope, save money as we haveto do many things in future that is why I ask you to get married soon. I said O.K Gauri dont try to become grand mother. I will talk to you after two days so good by and take care.

Next day ten in the morning I seated myself on Manager's chair and tried to think, what I have to do. Mr Terishkov has to deal with customers but before that I will have to answer their queries so I started familiarising with each product with their leaflets. I was astonished to see new models ofsour panel, air, gas, water turbine, hand and leg operated electric generaters, gas meters, surgical and home appliances, and so many otherv things conected with every field of life. There were miniature models, of indutrial machienery. It took me three hours to gain a primary knowledge of everything displayed there. Big industial units were to be demonstrated in the cabin computer by Mr Terishkov himself. I was busy arranging things when sounding horn Raju arrived. He embraced me and said I am in hurry but to buy some urgent goods for his tour, he had to come and without meeting me he could not go. Seeing the variety of display he took a round and was deeply impressed. He further said that he had been to Rampur to give the books Gauri had asked but she was not at home in stead he met Manish who took him to the fort on bike. Manish has done a marvelous job, of repairing and white washing the fort rooms. He also had made a small Godess temple on the roof top of the fort with a flag. Hearing all this I could not understand the need Manish had done at the fort. Raju than gave me three gift pack to me saying he had earned a lot in an Amerikan tour so he had brought these gifts to present Tanya, Juliyen and Terishkov uncle. He wanted to give them personaly but he had to go back immediately. With a promise to come soon he went back sounding horn. At about two o clock, Terishkov uncle arrived with his baggage from hotel to live on the tent prepared for him and to help me in organising the process of coming exhibition. Tanya and Juliyen were with him. I have arranged chairs for the interview. When I presented them the presents Raju had given me. For Terishkov, a Rajasthani Hukka and earings for Tanya and Juliyen. They had not expected this type of presents and that too from Raju a new comer, so were over whelmed. With pleasure they accepted and thanked Raju for his thoughtfulness. At three o clock only ten girls came and Juliyen started asking general knowledge questions about the products displayed in the exhibit. I saw that Juliyen had done her homework well. By participants way of talking and their gestures, she sent them to Terishkov uncle one by one to the cabin. In an hour four girls were selected and were given approval to join us from next day for practical demonstraion. We all seated in the cabin began to discuss about the problem of two demonstraion girls which we could not select. Tanya suggested that they had completed their research work, notes have been made and only the typing work was left. Why not we request Juliyen to accept the offer and do the typing here at spare time. It will be a monetary help to her also. Juliyen agreed but said she will agree to it in only one condition and that too if Tanya joins her. I suggested to uncle that if in demonstration one American and one Russian foreign girls join, it will create a good impression on customers. Including me, we will be seven in all that will be sufficient. Tanya will help you in computer demonstration. Tanya had no way to object so she too agreed. The problem solved Terishkov uncle smilingly looked at the girls and said this is for the good, I dont have to worry for them any more as they will be near with me all the time. It was agreed that in next three days all demonstration girls will be trained to look after their accorded duties which will be to advertise the products displayed before the opening on fourteenth Novembar.

Next day at elevan the training program started. I with Juliyen deputed four girls to each row and with the

help of descriptive leaflets guided them, to understand the
products displayed on the tables. Any further queries were
to be forwarded to me only and from me to Terishkov
for finalizetion. Tanya was busy with uncle Terishkov in
understanding computerised demonstration of industrial
units. Remembering the dresses I advised all the
demonstration girls to select Indian silk dress of Sari and
Blouze which they immediately approved. Tanya and Juliyen
had to be convinced that they will look more beautifull in
Rosi coloured Sari and Blouze which were like Top and
Skirt but in a large size. With hesitation they agreed. When
they put Rajasthani earings and bengales all other girls
congratulated them for their appearance. Before opening, in
three days time we all were at ease, to see the girls enjoying
the task they had been given. On Fourteenth Novembar the
President of India at five o clock in the evening inaugrated
the World Trade Fair with proper pomp and show, along
with distinguished guests. As per program we knew that
first five days were reserved for bussiness people hence a
strict diciplin was maintaned. Juliyen at commond all the
girls behaved politely giving full attention to prospective
buyers. Most of the time Terishkov uncle and Tanya were
busy. Make In India programme and colabrations gained a
total bussiness of Rs. two thousand crores which Terishkov
uncle never expected. On seventeenth at lunch time Gauri
phoned me complaining I had not talked her to Tanya as
promised, I handed over the phone to Tanya, asking her to
speak with Gauri who spoke some Russian words to Tanya.
After that in mixed language they talked for some time.
Juliyen too spoke with Gauri in mixed Hindi and English.
They look pleased talking to Gauri. I too felt relieved for
Gauri getting two new friends to talk with. After five days

the Exhibition was opened for general public and the rush of spectetars began and we were busy all the time. Only at lunch time, I and Tanya both talked with Juliyen in Hindi, they both were good learner and with demonstration girls at hand, began to talk fluently. It was twenty eighth Novembar at ten in the night lying on the bed I was thinking that only two days were left for the exhibition, after that four five days to dismantle the Dome and I will go to Rampur for at least two months to rest and get Gauri and Manish married at the earliest before joining Oriental or to some where else. Mind busy at thinking I slept soundlessly and woke up at six in the morning.

As usual after eleven in the morning, rush of people began. Families, youngasters began to group around their favouriate items. That day I received only one enquiry. Demonstration girls were now at ease talking with each other. After lunch at about four in the evening Tanya and Juliyen busy talking the setelite phone began to ring. It was unusual. I heard Terishkov uncle talking in Russian and suddenly Tanya rushed to the cabin leaving Juliyen alone. After few minutes Terishkov uncle came out side folowed by Tanya and telling me to cancel all the enquiries, went to his tent hurriedly. Tanya too went with him. I had never seen Tanya going out in Saries. Juliyen was looking at me questioningly. Tanya had gone to the tent without telling her any thing. I too was worried but thought that if anything is wrong that concerns us Terishkov uncle will tell us in time. Juliyen looked worried too and went to the tent and returned back saying Tanya will stay in the tent to night waiting for some urgent call. She went back to hostel in auto rikshaw. Waiting and locking up at eight in the night, went to my tent. I could not consontrate on my prayers, went to canteen for dinner which was tasteless to night and slept waking many times. Next day at elevan in the morning Terishkov uncle came inside and sat down beside me in a chair. He looked as if he had not slept at night, and spoke to me slowly, Amitabh, do me one more favour, I have to go to headquarters immediately so cancle all the appointments and dont take any further enquiry. Saying this he went back to the tent. As usual people were taking round of the exhibits and going out. Lunch time came, all were present except Tanya and uncle Terishkov. Juliyen came near me and tears in her eyes whisperd Amit there is some bad news, I feel it in my bones. Please go and enquire. I consoled her saying look Juli I know that Tanya's mother and sister are safe. Juli asked, Amit how do you know? I said Juli try to under stand, no body hides this type of news from near ones, they straight way tell the news so please wait. If any thing that concerns us also, Uncle will inform in time. Please have courage. The weight of unhappyness had slowed the time. We felt that the time was moving very slowly. At eight o clock the exhibition came to an end. I paid the wages to demonstration girls and saying good by's they went home. Uncle Terishkov phoned me to wait inside the cabin with Juli. After some time Uncle with Tanya came inside the cabin and sat down on chairs. Tanya was in her previous days dress, with tear marks in cheeks. In just twenty eight hours uncle looked older than before. Waiting for a while, he said slowly, my children, I have some bad news to tell. It does not concern, my family, it concerns me, you and all of the whole world. Please keep it upto you. Dont tell any one. Dont whisper anything. Some time back a well known astronomical scientist Yuri Dimitrize was surveying the Jupitar when he detected an astroid which was going to colide with Jupiter. It was coming from outside way that was unusual because the Astroid Belt is between Mars and Jupiter. He thought it to be an Alien Astroid coming from some other Galaxy. It attracted his attention and followed its course. He was astonished to see that its tremendous speed is out winning the gravitational force of Jupiter. He continued the search and was rewarded when he found the Astroid emerging from the other side but its course had changed a bit. His computers calculated its course that was leading it to another colition with Mars. He named the Astroid Dragon, its speed has lessened a bit. Dimitrize calculated that this Dragon's movement is unusual and if the speed lowers much, it will move to another planet and that will be our own earth. Horror stricken he appealed to world scientists through chenal Elevan, The same chenal Elevan your sister Gauri was enquiring about. It became known afterwords that this Dragon colided with another Astroid before Mars that broke it into two parts. One went away but another in a new orbit is coming, towords us. Son you might have heard about an Astroid which was going to colide with Mars on Second Decembar. With big expectetions the scientist world over were waiting for this great event after Hally's Comet's endevour with Jupiter. The scientist were folowing its corse for months, they were sure that this Astroid will colide with Mars but unexpectedly it did not happened that way. Something unusual happened, it reached the spot of Mars late and the Mars had gone unhurt to its corse. Scientists are confused and they are searching the cause. It will take some time to understand but the change of speed had created a serious problem of life and death for us here at Earth. As the Astroids corse has changed, as per calculation it is moving towords Earth in a great speed. Now you can understand the danger we are to face in forty five days. My neibour and a good friend of mine at Ministry had warned me in advance to come home at short notice. We have not been able to contect Tanya's mother. I have a morel responsibility to help you also that is why I am telling you all this. Saying this Terishkov uncle became silent but fear ingulfed me, body hairs stud erect in fear. Horror stricken faces of Gauri and Manish jumped in front of me. But the thought that Gauri knew something about this gave me some strength. There was a possibility that she must have made plans in advance for future action. A sound atracted my attention and saw Juliyen sobbing holding Tanya's arm. Tanya too had tears in eyes. Horror stricken Juli was moaning and saying oh uncle there is no oneand no where to go for me.. I will go where ever Tanya goes. I have no body else in this world, no body. Sobbing deeply covering her face she sat down on the chair. Taking a deep sigh I asked please uncle can you tell me where that Astroid is going to land? Terishkov uncle began to tell that all the telescopes in Earth and space are following its corse. It will be known to public after some time. As per their calculaion it is going to strike at the Russia and Mangolia border.. Saying this he began silent. Shaking words coming from him were telling the truth of fear he was feeling. After a while he again asked son now tell me what are you going to do? Thinking for some time I replied Uncle we can do nothing but to face the challange when time comes. There is a small fort near us, which has survived, centuries earthquakes. A small portion of the same could be used for our survival. I am going to repair and strengthen them to fulfill our requirements. In Hindu mythology, there are tales of Pralay and how mankind was saved. Again I will go through it, Rest I will leave to God who has the Power to do anything and everything. Holiest of Holi in Mahabharat Lord Krishna had preached that do your work honestly and leave the result on God. Saying this I too became silent. Ther was nothing left for me to say. Tanya and Juli were listening, our concersation seriously. After thinkinf something Uncle again said son between here and Mangoliya border ther are Himalyan ranges and your chances of survival are better than us at Russia. Again he became silent. His bowed head and worried expresstion were telling the truth. I wanted to give him some suggestions but what? Suddenly an idea came into my mind and said Uncle, as you have said that we have more chances of survival than you at Russia than why dont you and your family stay here with us? As I have already said, about a small fort near us, where we all can live comfortably. With you around us will boost up our energy to face the chalange. Like a father you will guide and give directions to what should we do? Hearing my words suddenly he became alert as if gerked in sleep. Tanya and Juli too were looking at me in such a way that I felt, as if I have done something wrong. He stud up and embraced me saying I have heard many times of Indian hospitality but in such a time when everybody will be looking for himself, this type of sugestion had bewilderd me. Definately I will think over it and decide it by tomorrow. I have no words to thank you, atleast you have made a point, not only it has lessened the impact of sarrowfullness but it had reminded me a saying that success comes to those who dare and act, it seldom goes to timid. Once more he embraced me, Tanya and Juli too came to me and shaking hands showed their gratefullness. There was nothing left to talk about but to face the chalange bravely. With a strong will uncle along with Tanya and Juli went to his tent and locking up the exhibition gate and supresing my wandering fearfull thoughts I reached to my tent and bowing in front of Tridev God began to pray Oh almighty He Bramha, He Vishnu, He Maheshvar so me the way, guide me as to what I should do. I dont know how much time I was praying in this condition when the phone bell ringing jerked me to senses. With trembling words I lifted the phone and said hello. A voice replied Dadu I am Raju speaking from the closed gate. What has happened to your voice? For a sinking man a small heystock helps him. Perhaps God had heard me and to help had sent Raju to me. Running I went to the Gate and embraced him fiercly. Seeing my condition he bacame suspitous and sitting me beside him in the car he came to the tent. Continiously he was caressing my back said Dadu I have come and I have never seen you in this condition. Tell me what is the matter which is bothering you? Gaining a little strength I told him each and everything uncle Terishkov had discribed. Raju's face became white in shock but recovering fast he stud up and said Dadu you have been my idole, dont loose your confidence. We have vowed togather in life and death. This is not the time to sit idle, If God had prewarned you through uncle Terishkov means God wants to help you in advance. You have mantioned that Gauri had enquired about it with Uncle, it means Gauri knows something about it. Call her immediately. I began to blame myself for not understanding this simple thing, sitting idle, doing nothing. At the same moment the phone began to ring. Before I could lift the phone Raju grabed it and said I Raju speaking Gauri Didi and are waiting for your phone since long. My friend Raju had a God gifted speciality that he never looses confidence and immediately understands the situation and acts accordingly. To give shock treatment he understud the situation I was in and had consoled me. The ringing of phone had made him understand that to be of Gauri only and she is in fear. To give her courage he immediately began to say Gauri I am very sorry that as promisd I will come to you after tour and will come togather here at Delhi to meet Amit da, was not possible as America tour was cancelled and I had to come here at Amit Da's place. He is here with me and we know everything you may be talking about. Now dont panick and tell me from where did you get all this information? Good, Good now give me the details I am noting it. Writing down what ever Gauri told, he said Didi you dont worry at all. Arranging all the things within two three days we are coming there. You know Amit Da's fax number, what ever preparation you have done and you need it send the details by fax tomarrow morning. Saying this he put down the phone. I complained Raju at least I too should have talked to her. Raju said Amit da this is the time to work. Tell me where is the computer? Every second is pretious. We will have to learn and understand too many things and dont worry about Gauri. I have made her busy for the time being. After some time, she will phone again, and by that time you will be normal. We dont have to loose our temper. I am beguning to understand. Cancelation of American tour proves that the matter is serious. Taking Raju with me I opened the exhibition gate and enterd the cabin to oprate the computer. Sitting on chair I tried to search the Internet sites Gauri had told but was unable to clik any one. Then Raju began to try. We both were beginers so trying again and again. In the mean time we felt that some body is watching us and looking back we saw Tanya, Juli and behind them uncle Terishkov. They all were looking surprised, there was nothing to tell but I gave the list of websites to Tanya. Without saying any word, all of us sat down infront of computer's big screen and Tanya's fingers began to move fast. Gradualy what ever pictures and information we saw, stopped our breath, we all were perespiring. Planets, Astroids, Comets, extinction of Dynosours, earthquakes, Sunami, uptill now, we had heard about them but visualising it in front made us root stricken. At first Raju came in senses and said I salute to Gauri who alone, is bearing the load of terror for months. Our main hope depands on her only. He wanted to say something more when the phone began to ring. Tanya and Juli were startalked. I consoled them saying it is from Gauri. I switched on the speakers and said Gauri and she immediately began to complain Bhaiya you are cruel. I am fearing much, tell me when are you coming. I replied Gauri why to fear, it is the cause of not knowing something and when we know the things we have to face, we are prepared for that and will face challange strongly. Raju is with me and for your information Tanya, Juli and Uncle too are sitting here. She became exited and began to plead Bhaiya please let me talk to him. Since long I wanted to talk with him, to ask questions of my queries. I want to apolise for not being able to come to him, to pay my respect. It would have been a great pleasure for me to meet uncle Tanya and Juli but it is too late. Immediately uncle intervened and said honey, I did not know that you speak english so well otherwise I would have spoken to you earlier. You dont have to appolise, what you have done had made me realise that what danger we are in and what we shuld do to protect us. I salute your mother and father who had borne a brave child like you. As you know my wife and daughter are thousands of miles away from here, though I have already requested to one of my friend to construct a u type structure for shelter, but I am not fast enough to visualize. What more I should do. Honey will you suggest some more? Gauri said oh uncle, I have dreamt of being burn alive by volcanic bioplastic heat, being drowened by enormous sunami waves, being whisked by big storms crying to save Amit Bhaiya and Manish's life, I have experienced all those horrors, I pray to God that it should be a dream only, but as you suggest that it is going to happen soon I will suggest to be thousands miles away, where that Damon is going to land. Uncle, please, have you any idea, where that Damon is going to strike? Terishkov uncle were listening all this sustaining breath, than sais Honey as Amit knows, that Damon is going to land at Russia and Mangoliya border but its impact will spread all over the Earth. Hearing this Gauri began to say uncle please I am going to ask you a favour, will you obolise me please? Yes honey, uncle began to say I will give and do anything you ask for if it is in my power. Then uncle, Gauri said why dont you, mother, sis, Tanya and Juli stay here with us in India? There is nobody to look after us. With your support and guidence, we have fare chances of survival here. Am I asking you too much uncle? I had never heard speaking Gauri so politely and sincerly. Hearing all this Terishkov uncle became dumb and words spoken with full of emotion said Honey, youhave not asked for anything butyou have given me and my family something very valueable.. The samething your brother here asked for. Isit a coincidence that bratherand sister asking the same thing, Are the almighty has favoured me with such a caring and loving friends like you both. Uptill now I was undesided but now I am sure what I have to do. Yes we all will stay here with you. Tanya and Juli will stay here with you and I will go back to Russia to bring my wife and daughter. These words made Gauri so happy that forgetting english she began to speak in Hindi saying Oh uncle, living with you, nobody can harm us, whatever dificulties come in our way, we will overcome and gain victory. Tanya and Juli too became glad and smiling embraced me and Raju. Gauri said Bhaiya it is late now and today I am going to have a sound sleep. Tomarrow after nine we will not get a seconds time to rest. In the morning you will get all the information, requirements and responsibilities by Fax. Than till tomarrow, by and thanks uncle, Tanya and Juli. Gauri has disconected the phone but in our minds there was only one name GAURI.

CHAPTER 3

GAURI

I was very happy today. This day brings me many happenings of gladness. First because it was my birth day and secondly today Pushkar Tirth fair started and we all father, mother, bhaiya, Mani and his father whom we called Tauji go for a visit their and worship Lord Bramha. Mother used to tell that our father Shri Rameshwar Prasad ji and Tauji shri Dulare Prasad dubey lived at Shahpur village of Unnav district near Kanpur. They were good friends and to earn their living better they moved out of the village and wandering reached here at Pushkar Tirth. Hearing Lord Brmha's greatness, setteled here. In whole India His temple is here only, so who woulnot like to bath in Pushkar Tank and recieve blessings of Lord Bramha. I woke up early in the morning and taking bath and wearing good clothes sat down on wooden seat in front of small temple where mother used to worship. Father and bhaiya too came there. At first mother completed thei worshiping than she put curd and rice dot on my fore head and distributed sweets. Than came the joyfull moment father gave me Earth Globe, Bhaiya a book on science technology and mother gave me Rajasthani choli and ghaaghra. I was running here and there toshare my happyness with some one and show the gifts but Mani has not come so for. I was annoyed in mind and thought that I will not talk to him anymore. Instantely Mani arrived running and gasping, before I could complain he gave me a large Cadbury chocklet. My anger disapeared and I begin to show him my gifts joyfully. Mani was three four years older than me and class mate of bhaiya. I used to quarrel with him now and then but without him, none of my work was completed. Father and mother enjoyed our quarrels and snatching favourite things. At ten in the morning we reached at Pushkar by bus. Whole day long we enjoyed the fair and in the evening went to the temple to attend the ceremony performed in worshiping God Bramha. We returned back at night. Mani had purchased a flute in the fair and sitting on the terace began to learn making various sounds. I got one more chance to irritate him. I sitting on the verandah used to irritate him by making shriking sound. In the morning worshipping with mother than homework after that to girls school and at night gaining knowledge in different subjects was my daily routine. I was my father's darling and bhaiya was mothers. My father were chemestry teacher in school. When in the evening he came back from school, with Tauji they played chess. I regularly served them tea and snakes and sat beside them on a stul. As I sit Tauji gives me a choklate and flavouring it I watched them playing. Tauji had big mustache which i liked much. Sometimes coming or going he touched his mustache to my cheeks and I giglled and they too enjoyed laughing. On holidays with bhaiya and Mani we played card, caromboard and ludo. In summer vacation Raju bhaiya used to come and we all went to the farm on bycycles. We climbed at the hill temple, surveyed the fort or dipping our feet in the tank, sang a song, Bachpan ke din bhula na dena. My days were passing this way in meryment. Anual exam were over. In father's school science practicals were in progress when accsidently a fire broke out in the lab. Father saved all the students but broken glass and fuming gases took the life out of him. Fire broke out in the school but our green pasture of happyness burnt down. As if a lightening had striked, mother became inert, sensless. Bhaiya became speachless, he sat beside her holding hand. Mani came many times, stud there looking at them unable to help. Tauji came and tried to console mother saying he will manage all the things in every way possible. Going back, he always hide his tears. Seeing our stricken faces, tears began to roll from mother's eyes. I forcibly talked her to divert her mind. Gradualy she became normal. Summer vacation has already started Bhaiya started going to Bhilwada saying he had got a job. He used to go early in the morning and came back eight in the night. Mother started sending me school forcibly. Tauji began to send Sukhiya chachi evening and morning to help household jobs. With his efforts mother got teaching job in the school. With in a year we received father's provident fund money. Cunsulting my mother Tauji admitted Bhaiya in Jaipur Enginering colege. Gradualy all became normal but once my childhood days were gone they never came back. My time began to spend on reading books sitting beside mother. The origin of human species, arctic, antarctic, conqering of mounteverest, Arya Bhatt, cladius Talmi, Kalidas, Vivekanand, began my favourite subjects. Reading them I felt near to my father. If I did not understand anything I tried to get the answer in the books itself. Mani used to come daily to meet mother. Seeing him mother always talked with him lovingly. Tauji started coming again to our house. The same way table was set for chess, tea was served, choklate given to me, he played chess for both sides but inhaling deep sigh of sarrow, damping tearfull eyes went back. Mani was not consantrating in Grain shop so Tauji got him admitted in Bikaner Agriculture College, thinking learning new mathods he will earn his living better in future. I heard that Raju Bhaiya too has gone outside for further education. Two years passed this way. One day evening when I was busy reading a book I was attracted by a sad flute tune. It seemed to be heard before too. It was singing AAja tujhko pukare mere giit re, mere mitwa. I could not wait, looking out I saw Mani playing flute sitting on the porch wall. Tears began to roll my eyes, with love and happiness, I called out loudly Mani when did you came back. Next day Bhaiya too came back from colege in vacation. Coming he embraced me kissing my forehad asked how is my loving sister. He has gained his full height of six feet. He looked matured with improved personality. Time heels all wounds. Now as usual at morning religious songs, after noon news and at night

Discovery, National Geographic on TV, began to entertain us. Bhaiya of eng. college, Manish about agriculture and I began to tell our experience and views. Tauji began to teach them, chess and wanted to know and discuss their future plans. Looking to our secured future, mother's confidence began to rise. After vacation Bhaiya went back to college. Tauji had handed over his agriculture land to Manish and had purchased two bulls necesary for cultivation. Our land was given on share to gain rice for a year. Other expenses were met by mother's pay. Time was moving fast. In two years by producing thrice of what they were getting before, Manish had surprised Tauji and closing his grain shop he began to help Manish full time, managing guiding him regarding seeds, fertilizer etc. One day when he came, began to tell mother that alongwith Amit, Manish too had achieved his goal and he is fully satisfied, God bless them both. My school exams were just over when a serious incident happened. In the forest, searching for bulls, serpent, bited Tauji, in saving Manish. Taking him to hospital by bullock cart, became late and Tauji died leaving us alone weeping. It was again a serious blow. Bhaiya rushed to Rampur from college. Till all the funeral function of therteen days, he never left Manish alone for a single minute. Forcibly he fed him and tried to console him. His relatives came from U.P Mother did all arrangements without bothering expanses. Mother and Sukhiya chachi showed great pasions. Mother never became disturbed. Curling Manish told you are as good a son to me as Amit and Gauri. From today onwords all responsibility is mine., Doing a mervolous job at the farm you have so much pleased and satisfied your father not so many could do. From to day wont you call me mother? Hearing this Manish embraced mother shading tears. Mother agreed Manish to take his tea breakfast, lunch and dinner with us and went home with Sukhiya chachi to sleep. One day mother asked Manish to visit his farm, he became glad and immediately brought an autorikshaw. I was surprised, as mother had never taken intrest, in the farm activities. I thought now what has happened to mother but could not get any answer. We all went to the farm happily. Mother standing on the raised ground served all minutely, asked questions with Manish about fields, tank, dairyfarm, prodution avrage etc, and said Manish you are doing well here but you lack one thing, for getting your efforts value. Why dont you erect a Tube well? I will take bank guarantee and bear the expanses, alongwith you will look after my agriculture land too. Tell me if you are agree. Manish wanted mother's affection and times bussyness to oercome his sadness. He immediately saying Maa embraced mother. I too had tears in my eyes looking to his happyness. His flute, begin to sing happy songs. I had passed my high school and taken admition in college. Taking mother's permission had also joined newly opened Rathore uncle's Siber cafe. Mr, Iyanger a Madrasi computer enginier taught us. I was astonished to see him taking pains in teaching us and sometimes thought how it is that he is working in a small town like Rampur. But seeing my willingness and active mind he gave me more attention and within six months I began to guide my fellow friends. I learned fast about e.mail. web searching, surffing etc. In the mean time Bhaiya had come back from Jaipur taking eng. Digree and after some days joined Oriental Fabricater. Her dreams fulfilled mother was happy. With in months Bhaiya gave me, gifts of a teltphone in our house and a mobile for my personal use. I became happy and busy all the time. All of asudden Mr. Iyanger left the service and went to chennai to join a big company. He had advised uncle Rathore about my ability and enthusiatham before so Rathore uncle came to mother and asked to help him, to send me as computer instructer and offered five thousand selary increasing every year. I personaly was not in favour of girls working but the attraction of Internet was too much so I agreed. Being myself local the number of learners increased and in spare time, as if I had gotten Ali Baba's Jinn the world seemed to be in my grasp, revolving at my commond. With a clik I began to get answer of unsolved questions of solar system, anotomy, risurche on human geens etc. Index file began to fill in my notebook. My daily routine changed altogather. I had enterd at my adolescence age. Manish too had done remarkably in agriculture production. Bank loan had already been paid. He had bought a bike also. When we met at night for dinner with mother, we always talked on various subjects. Manish was surprised at my general knowledge aquired throgh computer. I used to tell him about geofarmalogy and hydrophnics.cultivation. As per Bhaiya's suggestion he had purchsed two cows and asembeled a Gobar gas plant. From some where he had brought two puppies to grow and watch his fields. Once when Bhaya came he talked with mother about my marriage, my cheeks became red and I ran to another room. I could not think of marriage. Time became too short for me. It was moving very slowly. Month of July came. Manish was too busy in his farm. New admition were in progres and mother too had to spend much time in school. Ninth July evening when mother was returning from school which was not for off, a sudden rain drenched her and she had high fever at night. I and Manish became afraid. We immediately phoned Bhaiya at Gujrat oil refinary where he was at that time. By the time he came, we had consulted a local Doctor, who had prescribed some medicine. Mother had devloped some breathing problem. Bhaya was shocked to look the condition. He immediately called a Specialist Doctor from Jaipur. He came and investgated properly and declared to be a Nimoniya. He prescribed madicines but said to be carefull. Being mother a heart paitent it was not good. Forgetting everything we three took turns to look after mother. Second day she looked better, could not sit herself but we saw an strong will on her fece. When Manish had gone to purchase some medicines Mother called us both near her and began to say, you both have become matured and understand your responsibilities well. I wanted to get both of you married and complete my duties of well being but I dont know what the almighty had decided for me. I want to tell you about a promise your father made to lala ji before Gauri was borne. They both had decided that if I gave birth to a girl, she will be married to Lala jis, son that is Manish so that both the families will be bound togather in everlasting friendship. I want to fulfill your father's wish. My heart beat is bothering me and si I want that Gauri and Manish should be married to day only in front of me. Now tell me you both Will you fullfill my desire to day? Bhaiya thought it for a moment and smilingly answered, Mom thinking all childhood activities done by them, nothing can be better than this but have you asked Gauri and Manish? Mother looked at me. My cheeks became red But I said Mom, Manish had been my childhood friend and I like him too but have never thought this for. You get well first than I will do whatever you wish. Bhaiya too approved my saying than asked about Manish. Mother smiled weeklyand said, when Manuish became successfull in agriculture farm one day Lala ji came to me and asked me whether he should arrange marriage of Manish soon, as he is setteled now. I understud his meaning and I made him an offer, if Manish is agree? She will be too glad to marry Gauri with Manish. He became glad and next day had replied in affirmative. Mother told Amit Bhaiya to go and bring Pandit ji who informed that day was not suitable for marriage function but Tilak ceremony could be done. Seeing mother's condition and her wish next day Bhaiya arranged all the necessary things, invited near ones and in traditional way Pandit ji inviting Tridev God for blessings completed the Tilak ceremony. I was vowed to Manish. We were astonished to see mother's enthusiasom. She enjoyed it. When, photogaphed, between Manish and me, she looked happy. No doubt, it was a happy occasion. It would have been much more better, if done, when mother was well. Bhaiya, Mani, Me and Mother all smiled in diferent poses. By the evening mother looked exhasted. She called all of us to be near with her. Taking our hands turn by turn in her hands looked to be as if she was getting some strength. Before going to sleep she once more called us and gave blessings wishing a happy and prosoerous life. She slept soundlessly and never woke up in the morning. All hell broke up in the morning. We three were weeping continuously, embracing her, blaming ourselves, for not taking care for her properly. No body belived her passing in this way. All employies of the school, students and neighbours gathered in her funeral giving homage standing two minutes in silence. Any how Bhaiya completed all necesary duties of funeral. All the time he gazed towords mother's bed quitely. Manish from him to me and from me to him was trying hard to console us. I was in a shock. Sitting in front of Tridev God I asked questions, Oh God, what are your intentions? Why are you taking away our dear ones one after another? My all questions became unanswered. In lifes maze I could not understand whether God is punishing us for something wrong we had done in past or He is testing us, testing us for what that has to be seen in coming days. Mr. Vasudevan immediate boss came to pay homage to mother and giving example of Gita tried to console Bhaiya and made him readyto join duties for the welfare of family.

Bhaiya went to Gujrat to join duties, Manish became busy in the farm and I with heavy heart began to go Siber Cafe. Sukhiya chachi now lived with me. Manish went to farm in the morning taking his tiffin and returning in the evening did market purchsing. Till dinner he was with me trying to divert my mind, asking questions about various problems he may face. After losing father, Tau ji and Mother one by one my mind became suspicious and minor things began to irritate me. I began to see Indian, BBC, Cnn, and Masko news chanels. News of accidents, floods, earthquakes began to afraid me. I began to feel and imagine myself, with Bhaiya and Manish amidst, those happenings. and how to save us from them. Whenever at home, sitting alone began day dreaming. Seeing my condition, to keep me engaged, from farm brought cows, calves and pupies here at home. Sukhiya chachi engaged me in preparing breakfast items salted and sweets. Sukhiya chachi was too glad to be with cows and unknowingly I too had to help her in cleaning and feeding the cows and calves. Pupies began to come inside our room and I had to attend them by playing. Gradualy I came to my senses. To overcome my pressure of imaginary things I made up my mind to learn and do new things. To save ourselves from diferent happenings, ideas, bigane to make my mind strong and willfull. In place of terror, my will power started growing. I began to enjoy making future plans. Manish became glad observing my changing mental condition. All accounting and future plans he began consulting with me. I willingly cooperated with him taking intrest. Once again I began to enjoy things. One day evening about eight in Siber Café, surfing at random, a programme of Russian private chanel Elevan, attracted my attention. With a computer model the Presenter was showing different Planets and trying to explain something. Touching Jupiter's orbit line, he was showing an Astroid which was coming from behind and was merging in the Jupiter than after some time again it was emrging from the other side changing direction, moving towords another

Planet Mars than again it was coliding with Mars and changing direction seemed to be advancing towords earth. After that he showed some rockets fired from earth. Another picture, of its coliding with earth and blasting, huge pieces, falling on Earth, creating destruction every where. Showing these in several picturs the presenter was trying to explain something. Unable to understand the Russian language, I could not make up my mind as to what was that all about. Was it all imaginary or had already happened in the past or is going to happen in future. Frightened, this programme diverted my thoughts towords space. I started searching in my old books and notebooks. Western scientist has calculated earth's age to be forty six million of years. As per Abe Jorge Limatre's bigbang theory, trilians of year before, the universe was in a minute solid pressed round object and in due course inside pressure mounting, it blasted, dividing it in thousands pieces which spread out in the universe at a fast speed creating milky way. As per britishe scientist these milky way are still moving away but their Ghanatv is the same. In twentieth century amerikan scientist Adwin P.Hubal declared that these milkyway are in millions of number. In these, there are trillions of small and big different types of Stars. As per time new stars come in existance and old ones by eruption destroyed. Our Solar system is situated at the end of one such Galaxy. All these are bounded by internal Gravity and revolve around their prescribed orbit from one to hundreds of year time as per their solid or gas construction, revoling on their axis. Unani philospher Cladius Talemi in 146AD declared Earth as its centre and sun and other planets moving around the Earth. This theory continued 1400 years as Bible of Astronomy. In the year 1543 Polish astronamer Nicolus Copernicus vouched for

Sun centerd theory. Church rebuked this theory. but in 1642 Italian Gelilio Gelili with strong evidence approved Copernicus theory which is still in practice. As per latest calculation Earth moves around the Sun in 365 days 5 hours 48 minutes and 45 seconds. Mars planet in 687 days and Jupiter in 11.9 years, complets one round of the Sun in their orbit. When the Earth came into existance, it was in the shape of burning fireboll moving around the Sun like other Planets. Gradualy in thousands of years it formed into, thick hot lava. Earth's moving around motion in great speed in its axis accumalated heavy metal like iron in its center and lite metal came upwords. Steam, corban daioxide, methane and other gases spread into the atmosphere. Steam cooling down began to fall in the form of water. In millions of years, lava cooling down formed the upper crust which in due course formed islands and continents. In millions of years these continents are floating in samy liqid form of lava and moving upwords at the rate of twenty cm every year. Some scientists say that in that period an important incident happened. When the Earth was in samy liquid form, a small portion was pulled out of the Earth in space by gravitational force of Sun and begn to move around the Earth that is our Moon. Another theory says that a small planet colided with samy liqid earth that threw out a small portion into the space which became our moon circleing the earth as satelite. Comets tails consisted dried ice and vapour which colided with Earth in large numbers and in chemical reaction water fiilled in vacant space that formed oceans.. Gradualy the Earth became cool enough that life started taking shape in sea itself. Analis named millions of criimi object breaking carbanic yogik ineased the leval of oxygen in the atmosphere and life started taking shape in sea and land in the form of plants, trees and small creatures. Gradual development in millions of years man came into existance as homo sapians. In life circle man under his devloping ability is supreme. From Stone age man, looking at sun, moon, and blinking stars in the sky, felt wonder of their existance. When the Ice age was over, as per their developing ability winning the prevaling conditions, man spread out, in all the world. Killing birds and beasts, eating seasonal fruits, man devloped the skill of producing grains and started living in groups beside rivers. Frightened by nature's lightening, floods, earthquakes, volcanos man began to worship it naming God. Main worshiper and strong man started being worshiped. They began to be called kings and thus started Kingdom. Religon based kingdoms constructed Pyramids of Ezypt and Maxico, Giza memorial, Inka dynasty and others. All thesr were made consulting Sun and Moon direction. India, china and Mishr civilization are the oldest. In vaidic culture Time is devided in four catagaries. 360 days = one man year. 432000 man year = one Kaliyug. 864000 man year = Dvapar yug. 1296000 man year = Ireta yug. 1728000 man year = Satyug. 4320000 = one Mahayug. As per Vishnu and Bhagvat Puran universe age had been established at Four Arab and thirty two crore of years. The time left is to be half of what is said before. After that Earth's gravity will end and the Sun's severe heat will destroy the Earth. That will be the Pralay.

Reading all this I became glad knowing that the Pralay the end of Earth is for off but the gladness was shortened when I rememberd the incident by which Earth satelite Moon came into existance. As per Big Bang theory there are trillions of stars in the universe of which the stars who had completed their time explode and the matter is spread over in the universe. Latest discovery indicates that between Mars and Jupiter 6.5 million km away, is an Astroid Belt where thousands of Astroids in the shape of an small stone to hundreds of K.M. long bis stony form are moving around atracted by their gravity. When they colide, they change direction and fall down towords another Planets gravity. The craters seen on the Moon surface are example of these happenings. There are hundreds of Galaxies in which thosands of Astroids are wandering and coliding with each other if they are thrown out of their Galaxy, these Alien Astroids move to another Planets gravity and falling down create destruction. Jupter's gravity is tremendous and most of the Astroids are pulled down by Jupiter, In Indian mythlogy Jupiter is called Guru as it saves us from the attack of these alien Astroids, most of the time. Scientists have been able to locate fifty percent of these Astroids of which two hundred of these are big enough to do damage to the Earth. It is a complecated method by which scientists locate their where abouts and in the case of an Alien Astroid it is rather impossible to locate them and do something. In the Earth itself hundreds of craters have been discoverd wher in past Astroids had fallen. In 1993 at Etaly, space Guard Foundation came in existance to search these Astroids. In Huston at Amerika a labotary has been established to invent the method by which these Astroids could be diverted to another course or to destroy them safely. At night we see stars falling to the Earth, actualy they are small stony objects coming from space. When they enter earths atmosphere they get heated up and burn down. Tons of these particles fall down every day. Six and half miilion years ago a ten k.m. astroid hit at Ukretone Maxico that created hundred fifty km. wide crater. By impact the erupted dust, smoke and heat engulfed the whole world for months resulting extinction of Dynosours. At that time the Earth was full of forests and the oxyzen leval was above 40% plus the fertilized flora made Dynosours so big. The burning of forests increased the leval of corban die oxide increased, oxyzen decreased and suffocated at first the vegitation and afterwords Dynosours died. Only those creatures survived who were under ground or were in sea. On 30 june 1908 in Tungrska at Siberia an Astroid blasted in mid air resulting 1500 sq. miles forests were destroyed and its boom was heard upto six hundred km. 14 june 2002 a big Astroid passed through at a great speed beyond moon at a distance of one and half miillion k.m. away. Coming from sun direction it could not be seen. After words it was located. On 18 march 2004 and 15 janvary 2008 too Astroid passed through at a distance. 31 May 2013 astroid named 1998 qb2 at a distance of 5.8 million km. away 2.7 km wide again passed through at a great speed, it was one third of the diameter which finished the life of Dynosours from Earth.

In the process of reading about astroids, doubts began to rise in my mind and frightened, closed all the books and fell down on the bed thriving and began to think that is this the way humans are going to wipe out of the earth. The thought that scientists are busy solving the problem gave me some assurance. Hubal and Chandra like too many telescopes are searching the skies twenty four hours a day by which scientists will know in advance about these astroids, and comets who may colide with the earth. They are making plans to divert or destroy them in space so that we may be safe. Thinking that I am not alone but thousands of scientists too are busy in finding a solution gave me some strength. and I was busy again in my daily routine. In chenal elevan only local news was shown nothing new about astroids. One night during diner Manish asked me about a problem he was facing in determining the spot where he wanted to build a grain store, he further told that mother wanted that they should built a house there too. He wanted to know whether I will help him. I immediately agreed and on Sunday, with Sukhiya chachi reached the farm in autorikshaw. The road had become, broder shining with asphault, I can look at the Godess temple on leftside hill. Before the farm, road diped to a slope and continued upto Ahmadabad highway. Our farm was ten feet above the road. Entering the wooden gate on north at right side a pavement beside the lotus filld tank went upto the old Ramgadhi fort on west. On south small ridges, all around crop filld fields gave a peacefull impression away from the uproar of the town. Beautiful place, to live in realy. Standing on the cleared up space, where a small stony mound was, the cool murmur of the air, was thrilling me. Seeing me Manish came running and we discussed first about the grainstore which was to be built beside the cowshade, The cleard up space was good enough for constructing the House. I saw a changed form of Manish here at the farm. At home very often he talked about anything but here he was speaking continiously about his future planning and how he will do it. Looking to his happyness I agreed to all his praposals. Finaly it was decided that preparing a house map he will get it approved by the municipal commetee and when Bhaiya will come, with his appruval startthe construction. That night I received a phne call from Bhaiya who informed me about completion of the oil efinary at Gujrat and he was waiting at Delhi for another project. For several days I did not received his phone call and I began to worry. Whenever I phoned to his office at

Oriental, I was told to leave a massage for him. I had my mobile phone but Bhaiya did not liked to be disturbed all the time so had not purchasd any mobile. It would be very dificult for Manish to search for him at Delhi so I became more worried. By third Novembar I was so preturbed that I began to weep when at eight in the night when the phone rang I began to weep uncontrolably and complained mercilessly to him. He consoled me in soothing words and when he told me about his new job at the world Trade fare and his appointnment as manager I became glad in understanding that he will be near at Delhi now and we can meet him any time. He promised that after this job he will be with me for two months before going some where. All my complaints forgotten I felt a new energy believing now I will face all the challanges who came in my way. On eightth novembar Raju Bhaiya came sounding horn of his jonga jeep. He looked very glad. First he gave me my books which I had asked him and than began to tell in his jolly way about Bhaiya's new girl friend Tanya and Juliyen. He told me in detail about the picnic and dinner they both had with those girls. Every now and then I used to think about the lonliness of Bhaiya, here I had Manish to look after me and sukhiya chachi to talk about plus my Siber cafe to pass the time talking and searching the Internet but Bhaya was alone busy with the job and responsibility of mine. I became glad knowing he has some friends with him to fill the gape of lonliness. Second thing that gladend me was that his boss's daughter Tanya was Russian and making her my friend I will be able to know about the authenticity of chenal Elevan programme which was never away from my mind. On seventeenth Novembar I phoned Bhaiya reminding him about Tanya. She immediately began to speak in Hindi saying namaste Gauri ji how are you. I was surprised Tanya speaking so well in Hindi. I spoke only few words in Russian and was relieved in mind that now I will be able to talk with her freely about my doubts. At first I asked about her father's health than asked about chena Elevan. She replied that she certainly will ask her father about it and will inform me accordingly. Then I spoke, to Juliyen in few words. After that it was easy, we began to talk frequently. Tanya wanted that I should talk to her in Hindi only so that if needed she may make it a cerrior and we girls always have something to talk. One day she told me that her father knew about chenal elevan and he is collecting information about my enquiry. In a short time we knew all about their upbringing, educatio and future plans. Sympathising with each other, it seemed we all were traveling in the same boat, strugaling to survive in this cruel world. Tanya was too much impressed by Bhaiya, and always praised him for his devotion to work and faithfullness. Juli liked Raju bhaiya and she looked at his mustache lovingly which reminded her father whom she loved very much and had the same mustache but lost her parents in a car accident. She sympathised with Raju Bhaiya and was glad that he had good friends like us. She was too much upset being alone in this world except Tanya and was glad that in India she had made good friends like Amit Bhaiya, Raju and me. We three promise each other to meet on vacation and share happyness. on 23 novembar at night Tanya phoned me saying my enquiry about the Astroid was correct, his father looked exited. He had thanked me for the information and had said that the Astroid is moving towords Mars at a great speed. It is millions of km away. All the scientists are following its corse. There is nothing to worry for me but had advised to watch and get informaion from media. He will inform me future developement. She said Amit is with Dady she will talk to me some other time. I was relieved to know that including me, all scientists world over are watching astroids movement. I asked a question to myself that why this particular event is bothering me again and again. I could not say how much time I was busy in thoughts when Mani's voice jolted me to earth. He was waiting for the dinner with me. Holding myself I again tried to think over the talk I had with Tanya. I began to feel that something bad is going to happen and the Almighty God is indicating me to be prepared for the worst. Without loosing any time I should think about the welfare of Bhaiya, Manish, Raju bhaiya. We all togather have to face the challange if any. As per Tanya's information there was enough time but what will happen after that, nobody knows and by that time it would be much more difficult for me, to bear the load of that unseen, unpredicted future happening. I will have to share it with some one and that would be none other than Manish only. I decided that next day morning I will certainly consult with Manish in detail. That night I could not sleep well, for the whole night turning sides. Suddenly I rememberd, the telescope, which Amit bhaiya had sent through Raju bhaiya. I got up and going to the cortyard tried to focus it. Once mother had talked about Northstar and seven sisters so adjusting the telescope a little directed it towords sky. Thousands of shining stars came into view. In all direction, millions of stars. Any how, I was able to locate the nstar and seven sisters. I had heard about Mars shining red in the sky but trying hard I got exhasted. Thought about a saying that it is very dificult to gain new knowledge, without teachers guidance. Next day I slept late. This was unusual I always woke up at sunrise and after exercising Yoga for an hour did other duties so when I woke up at eight inthe morning, Mani had not gone to the farm but was walking up and down in the cortyard worriedly. Seeing me, he came to me hurriedly and asked whether I was not feeling well. I got ashamed and thought if at this time I am in this condition than what I will do when the time comes for action. With full determination I promised myself that to day I will keep Fast without eating anything and make future plans consulting Mani. Asked Mani to wait, requested Rathore uncle at Siber cafe for half days absence, took my bath and sitting in front of Tridev God began to pray. Souls strongness to day filled me with humbleness and devotion towords Almighty God that I did not ask him to give anything but give me strength and direction for my duties. What ever in return I will recieve. I will accept gladly. After completing my worshiping methodicaly, I started for the form sitting behand Mani's bike. I liked one of the qualities of Mani's nature most was that he never showed hurriedness. I felt that his devoted gaze made him understand what I needed that time. On way to farm we both were silent. Reaching there we both sat down beside the tank dipping our feet in the water. I was still silent. After a while taking my both hands on his hands Mani said affectionately Gauri I could not bear your minds torcher you are giving to yourself any more. Please unload it. With a deep sigh I narrated all from chenal elevan programme to the talk I had with Tanya and my minds feeling of something God given bad happenings. From childhood to the present incidents, of school's, of quarreling, of father, mother, and uncles death, I had never seen Mani disturbed but hearing all this, the result of terror, he was feeling, I can look on his face. Mani stud strong facing bravely each and every obsticles coming day to day but these out of his imaginaion's God given would be disaster, frightened him. Being silent for some time with shaking words he said Gauri since two three months through your behaviour and busyness I conected it with your worries of Amit Bhaiya but your continious reading of various books confused me. When you were expecting these type of God oriented events in mind, why did not you tell all this to Amit Bhaiya if not to me. Is there any reason behind this? I said Mani, there were two reasons. Bhaiya was working at Gujrat between heavy machines and this can divert his attention resulting an accident that I would not like secondly this would be event was going to involve whole of the world. Today's technolodgy has so much improved that scientists prophecy the end of sun and earth which is going to happen after crores of years. To save human species are making plans to migrate to another planet. If anything bad is going to happen, he would know it first at Gujrat between expert people there. I too doubted the chenal elevan programme but one after another death of father, mother and Tauji made my mind full of terror. Fear is the by product of unknowingness and to over come it there was only one solution and that was to gain more knowledge through books and console my mind. My rudeness towords you, i did not like myself. I once again wanted to forget myself listening to your lovingflute tunes but it seems the Almighty God has reserved someting else for us to do. Now tell me what we shall do. By this time Mani had become normal. but serious and started saying Gauri, Amit bhaiya will be coming after a few days and we will do whatever he tells us to do but in the meantime we should not sit idle. We have enough money in bank for the constructio of the house but that too will be invested as per his advice. Now tell me, as per your knowledge you have gained through books, what kind of this God threatened incident will be and what preparetion we should do, without spending too much, to save us in future. I thought over the question Mani had just asked than replied actual facts will be known to us after some time, but I can make some assumption, At night every body has seen stars falling from the sky with along shining tail burning behind but when ever any comet with long tail has benn seen it indicated bad happenings in the past and people were afraid of it. Now a big sized Astoid is moving towords Mars planet in a great speed. Every body has seen or read about Helly comets going to pieces and falling down in Jupiter. Every scientist in the world, are looking towords this fast moving Astroid which is going to colide with Mars with great expectations. Definately this is going to be a great event. Mani my own doubts are worring me too much. I feel that when Jupiter the biggest planet could not stop this Astroid how Mars, which is small in size than Jupiter, could stop or destroy the Astroid, and if it eluded the gravity of Mars than definately it will come towords us at Earth. Mani in books there is written that six and half crore years before an astroid 10 km wide ramed into the earth, creating hundred and thirty km wide crater, in ukretone Maxico. Its force erupted so much dust, smoke and heat that engulfed the earth for many years. All vegitation got burned and for want of food Dynosours were wiped out from the earth. Earthquakes and volcanos had destroyed many old civilizations. The tsunami started by earthquakes had drowned many sea side civilizetion also. Man's strong will and determination had not only saved him from disasters but made him stronger. In man's history the progress and discoveries he had made in last five or six hundred years had never been done in past. To days information technonlogy had made him so strong that not only he had reached moon but is trying to discover far away planets through robot setelites. Every night, falling stars look beautifull but their big vorsins had done very much destruction. Hundreds of craters have been discoverd where these small and big astroids had fallen on the Earth. In our Hindu Mythology there is a discription of Pralay when all earth was submerged in water. I will go through it again and try to know something of value. In todays condition, if we are to survive, the utmost need is to find or make a safe shelter where we can live upto five, six years, saving us from big storms, rains and floods, where we could keep our food and water safely for years. Mani, have you any idea about this type of a place? Mani thought it for a moment than standing erect, caught my hand and pulling it, invited me saying Gauri come with me. Pulling me ahead between fields, rising to the back of the fort, entering into the fort, climbed to the top of the fort and said Gaauri look at the six km. long small temple hill on East, spread over on west Aravali mountain ranges, thousands km. away Himalyan ranges on north, and on south east and west ghat ranges, I have seen and visited forty, fifty km. of sarrounding land. At Bikaner Agriculture college, when ever I used to think and remember you and about my home on vacation I traveled by bus to for off places. I walked on foot upto Jaisalmer. Heard many stories about sands encrochment by seniors but to day I feel that this place under the holy Pushkar Tirth shade, like this Ramgadhi Fort, I have not found any safe place. I have seen every corner of the Fort. Seeing your mental worries I used to tire myself in field work and some times by flute singing perhaps tried to call you. Saying this he uncoverd a stone and took out the flute, I saw written on the stone Gauri. Tears began to roll my eyes and forgetting all my sarrows embracing Manish sobbing I said Oh Mani, my beloved friend, realy I have been too cruel to you, I think I am like this since childhood, I have always worried you, but without seeing you, without quarreling with you I could not live. My eyes always searched for you, ears always waited for your voice. Mother's praposal of marriage with you i did not feel unusual it was like a rite for me. To day I feel that I have been blind in my selfishness and had done injustis to you. Oh Mani, my dearest childhood friend, please forgive me. Mani was affectionately sliding his hands on my back. When my sobbing was lessened he began to say Gauri what is fear I do not know. I have spent many nights in vacant palaces, in forests and in the desert alone. In forest where that poisionous snake bited father. I did not feard but the disaster you are talking about has made me terror stricken. Fear is the product of unknowingness. The more we know about it willlessen the fear. You will be ready mentaly and physycaly to face the challange strongly. You have done good, by unloading your worries and shared it with me. If this disaster comes, it will be a question of life and death not for us only but for the whole human being. With full heart we should prepare ourselves. From to day you go through in detail, writing everything we will need in future, I will try my best to fullfill it. As for shelter this fort seems to me strong but time must have left its impression on it in some places, so from tomarrow I am going to examine and repair it in a way to face big storms and rains. Remembering God, let us start by measuring it by counting steps in each room. You note it down so that we have a fare idea of space to be utilised in future. Doing all this, I understud that Mani was rite. Three feet wide stony walls, arches and beams made it a strong fort. Three big rooms, kitchen, toilet and a small cortyard were sufficient for our living purpose. An eight feet diameter dried well too was there. I became sure that after proper repairing and white washing, it could be a good shelter home. There were enough ventiletar for air and light. Encouraged we moved to backyard entrance which was conected with cowshed and a passage to field below. At about two in the afternoon we came back to the farm. To ease my mind Manish said that the disaster may come or not, he will get all repairs done in a weak. Do inform Amit Bhaiya about this. To day night we will discus again and prepare ourselves methodicaly. Rest we leave on God.

Coming back from the farm, Mani had gone to market and I rested for a while than went to Siber Cafe. Getting a safe place for shelter had increased my morale. Unloading my worries to Mani, I was feeling light hearted. The Cafe activities were normal but the time approching eight, my heart beat began to rise. with trembeling hands, I started chenal elevan. There was no news of coming disaster. I was surprised, media always dramatised every event, how small it may be, but the event which was going to be a question of life and death for all had not been mantioned at all in this programme, made me think that I might had seen a Dream of that event or it was only my imagination. Thinking all this when I came out of the Cafe, I saw Mani waiting for me. I ran to him feeling good and thought that what ever dificulties come in future Mani will guard me strongly lika a shield. Reaching home I worshiped dutifully and to break the Fast took some fruits and we both started making the final sketch of the fort we had measured in the morning. By the time it was finished I was feeling tired so leaving the rest for next, went to sleep. A terrible dream of myself flying in a great storm, Bhaiya and Mani strugaling to save their life in stormy waves of sea, awakened me. I was perespiring a trembaling in fear. It was four in the morning and a thought about people saying that dreams of morning come true made me so nervous that I immediately wanted to phone Bhaiya. A second thought came that if any thing new has developed, I will get it first from Tanya. It will be not good to worry bhaiya now. By Gods grace and our efforts we have found a suitable shelter and will collect enough food, water and other necessary things but will they be sufficient in saving our lives if that disaster came. Again and again this question came into my mind but I could not get any satisfactory answer. Suddenly I rememberd an answer I had replied of a question asked by Manish telling him about an incident that ended Dynosours from earth, crores of year back and in shock I sat down on the bed frightened. Oh God Almighty, do we all human species have to die like Dynosours. Some where in the books it must have been written, thinking this I began to search it pulling out Year Book, Readers Digest and other books conected with Astroids from Bhaiya's almira. It was seven in the morning when Hira and Ruby's barking, I came into senses. Usualy I woke up at six in the morning, did my Yoga for an hour then worshiping and breakfast, I gave milk and bred to Hira and Ruby, played with them for few ninutes. Before I went to siber cafe at nine, I did my studies to appear for graduation, privately. Sukhiya chachi had gone back to her native place leaving the job but she had engaged another woman to attend house jobs. Returning back at twelve from Cafe I was again busy searching about Dynosours. Scientists were confirmed that in Jurasic era Dynosours died due to air polution and lack of vegitation which broke the chain of survival. The origin of life started in sea and in due course spread over on land. Plants developed a chemical reaction of photosynthesis by which they converted sunlight and corbondiaoxide into oxyzen and sugar. They consumed sugar as energy and released oxyzen into the atmosphere.. The sun through light and heat has been the source of energy for all living beings. Millions of years back that astroids coliation with earth created a complete smoke filled darkness on the planet for years. In the absence of sunlight at first the plants and afterwords dynosours died by hunger. This search made me visualise in imagination that no earthquake, no volcanic eruption only lack of sunlight and oxyzen made dynosours extinct from earth. My first day was spent on Dynosours. Second day I tried to gain some new knowledge about geography and Botany. From time unknown trees and plants have been serving all living beings by producing oxyzen and supplying food and shelter. Not only they saved earth erosan, but supplied various medicines too. It all depande on sunlight. The earth takes a year to complete its orbit around sun that makes changes in temprature and forming seasons. The earth bending twenty three and half digree on exis creates six months darkness in north and south poles. It means the tree and plants had devloped an imunity to survive in that period. It means in jurasic era, the darkness prevailed, more than one or two years that ended the life of dynosours. Scientists discovered one more incident at Sumatra island wherethousands year back a super volcano erupted.that causedthe same effect of destruction on nearby islands upto Asia and Astralia. In Earth's life these type of disasters had been a process of event that will be continued in future. Thousands of species have become extinct but thosands have survived too. Reading all this only one thought came into my mind that Life and Death is all in the hands of Almighty God. I dont know how He looks, what shape He is in but I am sure that He loves us. He teaches us to be humble, to love all the creatures and plants He has made. He teaches us that what we will sow, we will reap. In Hindu Mythlogy when Lord Krishna, as a small child was playing in his mother Yashoda's cradle, He has laughingly shown her the Universe in his mouth. He has shown her His emense image with full decore. The latest discovery the scientists have approved is the Big Bang theory, conforming universe in a tiny small particle and expanding, engulfing in a Black Hole. I came into a conclution that this is the region of religious actions. In millions of years continious gradual devlopment man had made him so strong that either he will destroy himself or to save human geens, will win over new planets in universe. I began to understand that what ever happens in future, we should be prepared for it. If we have made preparation in advance, the success will not be for off. I felt in mind that how big that disaster may be, we will face it with strong determination.

I woke up early in the morning and had aleady decided today's activities for noting down coming years necesities. I started writeing, it was sure that sooner or later some God given disaster will take place therefore we should devide all the necesities as per their requirements. At present we have the time to think and decide for our needs otherwise nothing will be left but repentance in our hand. First and foremost we must have two shelters with full amentities, an uderground basement to save ourselves from heat and storms second one at a height to save us from heavy rains and floods. Second necesity-- Drinking water- without food we can survive twenty thirty days as per our health but without water in three four days we will feel weakness and our mind becomes hazy. We will not be able to consuntrate on anything so an average of two liters of water per day, per person comes to seven hundred liter in an year. At least we will have to keep in stock two thousand liters of water plus water purification unit and chemicals to purefie the rain water for future demands. Third is food. We have to colect two types of food, first one as ready to eat like biscuits, dried fruits, salted mixture, ground nut etc, which will be used only when we have no time to cook and second one which we cook like rice, pulses, wheat and other grains. To prepare our food we will be requiring gas sylander, oil stove, coal, firewood for future. Fourth - Light and Air - If we are to live in a darkend closed shelter for months, we must have torch, lantern, genrater, chargeble battery, hand charger etc plus ventilation facility. Fifth is Yoga. In a limited space to keep ourselves fit nothing is better than Yoga, a hours exercise will keep our mind and body fit. Sixth - Religious and other books - To give moraly strength the books will play an important roll in passing the time fruitfully. Seventh - Game and sports - Indoor games like chess, playing cards, ludo etc, will save us from boredom. Eighth - Radio & mobile - these modern gadgets will entertain you if you have battery charging facility. Nineth - Future requirements - If the disaster is so severe that you are pulled back to thousands of years back conditions, you will require all the necesities, you are enjoying today. You will not get all but atleast you will need warm cloths against cold, utensils, sufficient match boxes, lighter, carpenter and mason tools and firearms and other weapons to safeguard yourselves from criminals and wild animals. Writing all this in general I began to write what myself will need in future. Including me, Amit bhaiya, Mani and Raju bhaiya, we are four but in the time of distress some more person may join us and to be in safe side I will prepare my budget for ten persons, assuming the dificult time may exceed, beyond our expectaions. Daily requirements of food for one person - 150 grams each of Rice, Wheat and Vegetables, 50 grams pulse. For six years it comes to 3500 kg rice, 3500 kg wheat and 1500 kg pulse. Vegetables that could be kept safe for months like onion, garlic, ginger, achar, dreid vegetable bury, spices, oil, butter made ghee, sugar, gud, tea, cofee, salt, milk powder, poha, satuva, futa chana, ground nut, tetra pack milk, medicines etc. in sufficient quantity. All these are to be collected as per availablity and packed properly. If the darkness prevailed more than six months, all the vegetation will be destroyed and when the conditions improved, it will take years to grow again. If we collected enough quantity of seeds of grain, fruits, vegetables and trees and the process of their growing, they will be helpfull for our survival. We have been using all modern facilities since long but if we are forced to live in stone age conditions, we have to be prepared for that with all knowledge and know how of every thing. If we are able to collect all books related to survival and made a group of expert person to live with, we will be fortunate. Put yourselves in those conditions and think for each and every minor material which can hamper your survival. If you think that whatever happens with others, that will happen to me than say goodby to Future.

In the evening when Mani returned from the farm I showed him the list and details I have written. At first he was shocked to read it and said I thought that we have to arrange only food stuff but you have noted down all that is requierd in opening a shop. I suggested him to go through all the items and scratch them if not usefull in those conditions. Manish again began to read and think one by one and at last holding my hands, becoming emotional said Gauri, you have been my idol since childhood and appriciated your cleverness but today I feel proud of you, not only you are clever but foresighted too. What ever you have written are usefull in one or another way. Crops are ready in the farm to be packed. The quantity you have mantioned I am going to double pack properly dried. The extra production I am going to sell in the market by which we will purchase all the things you have mationed in the list. Whenever Amit bhaiya phone o you, tell him all, hiding nothing. He has a rite to know now, what we are doing. Manish further informed me that he had completed the repairing work of Ramgadhi fort and white washing will be done next day. After reading my list Manish asked me about two queries of drinking water and basement, which he could not solve. A well was there but it was dry. Drinking water was a must so I too became worried and tried to think about filling the well by water. Suddenly I rememberd that in old days, rivers and tanks were the source of drinking water and the big tank beside the fort must had been built for the same purpose. It was to be seen if any arrangement could be done to fill the well from outside. Converting the well into a storage tank could solve our problem. When I told Manish about my suggestion he jumped in gladness and said Gauri why did not this idea came into his mind. Within two three days he will get the well cleaned and properly repaired. To fill the well with water he will do it by conecting it with their tubewell. Regarding basemeni he said that he is going to construct two rooms of 10x15 feet in basement, where they had made a plan to construct the house itslf. I began to feel that God is showing the way and we are moving forword step by step. After many days I had a sound sleep. When in the morning I woke up, I felt hopefull and silence every where. I could not imagine that this silence was an indication of coming disasterous storm. After Sukhiuya chachi had gone to her native place, leaving the job, I too had resigned from siber café to attend my house duties. I had my own laptop to entertain myself and search through various chenals. As usual at seven in the evening chenal elevan was tuned and I was busy in housework when breaking news, caught my attention and the pictures with english titels frightened me so much that I called out shriking Bhaiya.

CHAPTER 4

WHISHPER
OF DESTRUCTION

World trade fare has ended and there was a complete silence in whole area. I began to feel that whole world has come to know about the coming disaster and frightened they had hiden themselves in their houses. Before nine in the morning we all assembled in the cabin to recieve the Fax, Gauri had promised to deliver. With a beep, full scape papers written in Gauri's hand writing in hindi language, began to roll out from the fax machine. In it were, priority based preparation. Many questions and their, point to point, detailed answers. Raju began to translate it in English and continued speaking for a long time. Some time we became surprised and another time felt fear engulfing us. Yesterday night, the Internet site detail, which Gauri had sent, contained 2004 tsunami of Lanka and at Japan in 2012, volcanic eruptions, severe earthquakes, heavy floods and land slides, were eyes opening but the detailed informaion, we were listening now were full of prababalities. We had our own doubts in mind but as Raju read it, the happenings took the form of moving pictures in front of us. Some times Raju stoped speaking in horror and with trembeling voice, started speaking again. Coming disaster will be so terrible, it was beyond our imagination. Suddenly the phone began to ring that shook us all and looked at the phone frighhfully. Bracing himself Terishkov uncle lifted the phone. Hearing Gauri's voice we felt relived. Uncle thanked Gauri for sending the detailed information last night. He asked Gauri why this much quantity of grains and other materials will be needed and how she had decided the time limit for six years. He was speaking in english and Tanya was translating Gauri's hindi in russian to Terishkov. Gauri replied uncle what were the reasons, I dont know but the first assumption scientists made was wrong. Todays news papers and TV chenals had prominently publsized the news of Mars becoming safe from astroid coliation. One paper had said that by this event Mars expidition was withheld and will start again. No body has mantioned the facts about the changed astroid's course or whether it will colide with earth or not. Millions of years before an astroid colided with earth that destroyed the vagitation and dynosours and engulfed the earth in complete darkness for years. By volcanic eruption on Tova at Sumatra is.land, the darkness prevailed for months. My thinking is that if a ten, twelve km wide astroid colides with earth at a great speed, the vacume it will make on its way, will suck the dust and thich smoke and spread over the upper leval of atmosphere which will take years to fall down on earth. This will hamper the sun light coming to earth and there will be darkness every where. If I am telling some thing wrong please uncle pardon me, but try to think, if years to come, we have to face big storms, roaring tsunami waves, heavy rains and flood in complete darkness, what will be left. All crop fields, villages, cities, indutrial units, dam, power houses, all will be destroyed.

Most of the human beings and creatures will perish. Only those will survive who were in the rite place at the rite time and had prepared their selves to face tha chalange. Uncle I have read one more thing that every twenty thousand years Ice Age returns than were these the reasons, in past for coming of Ice Age? Will this disaster lead to Ice Age again? Gauri was speaking continiously, as if the mental terror she had been feeling alone for months, she wanted to free herself from it and the words are coming out of her mouth involentiarly. She said again uncle out of the prsent populaion, how many will survive, nobody knows and who ever will be saved what they will eat? In past when man lived in forests, he made his living, eating fruits and hunting but what we will eat? There will be no vegetation, no trees. no forests and no animals for hunting. It will take too many years to grow vegetation and trees. Only creatures living under ground and at sea will survive. From present we will be living in Stone Age conditions. There will be only one difference from past and that is, our mind full off knowledge and destroyed civilization but no food to live on. With our limited resources what ever we will be able to save, will have to be sufficient to save our generation. And uncle to day every thing is easily available but after this disaster what will remain saved to buy. To day we can buy every thing we need by money but tomorrow money will be like piece of papers. What ever we have to do, we must do to day only. Tomarrow will be too late. I dont want that what ever mental terror I have felt in last months, Amit bhaiya, Manish and Raju bhaiya too have to bear. Saying this sobbingly Gauri finished talking. A deep silence, prevailed in the cabin, we all were in a shadow of fear. Bracing myself I said to Gauri, sister, now you leave all the rest on me, by this time you must have withdrawn all the money from bank, With Manish you buy all the things you have mantioned in the list and phone me what I have to purchase here. I will reach there very soon. Tanya and Juli too are coming with me. Probably uncle too will join us with family in a short time. I will talk to you tomarrow morning till than saying by I put down the phone. Nothing was left totalk about. I began to feel, a sensation in my body, mind became alert prepairing itself to meet the chalange. Questios began to roll in my mind and I asked, please uncle, tell me, do all human species have to die like small creatures? Terishkov uncle thought it for a moment than said, son, you must have read some where that in 19th century, there was a posibility of cold war, where atomic weapons might be used so to save from atomic rediation, all big countries and their rulers made under ground shelters with full facilities. In Amerika and Europe thousands of rich people made fully furnished shelter, which are still there to use. Atomic rediation prevails too many years so proper food and water supply too was arranged accordingly. What ever your sister Gauri had said are all true. It is my good luck that God had given me a chance to meet kind hearted people like you otherwise, before he could complete his words, the satellite phone began to ring. We all seemed to be pairalised hearing satellite phone ring. Immediately uncle began to talk in russian, Tanya went near her father, Juli's face became white in fear, To under stand the effect of talk when I looked at Tanya, she was trying hard to stop tears that were telling the truth of unhappyness she was feeling. The talk over, Terishkov uncle closing his eyes sat motionless for some time than taking courage, began to speak in trembaling voice, son, nobody in this world can stop, what is going to happen. I have been instructed to return immediately to Masco. All foreigners have been told to go back to their countries. No reason, have been told, it will be announced after some time. Hubbal, Chandra and latest radiation detecting telescopes are monitering this astroids movements. Big powerfull rockets are being loded with bombs to destroy this astroid in space. World over scientists are busy finalising the method by which they can avoid destruction. Coming days are going to be very hazardous. He became silent again thinking, head bowed. Feeling Tanya's hand touch on his shoulder, he decided something in mind. He raised himself straight on the chair and opening a drawer, took out a cheque book, wrote something and gave it to me. I saw a cheque for Rs fifty thousand. I asked him, what was that for, he said till he returns back from Russia, he is leaving Tanya and Juli in my protection and to purchase needy things for them, he was giving me that cheque. I could not see his worried face so thanking him for his thoughts I returned the cheque to him and said, as I know Gauri, she will arrange and collect more than it is required for ten persons for ten or twelve years. We dont need this today, please keep it with you when you come back, if need be, we will use it. He took back the cheque but asked me a question that confused me and I began to think that he has last his mental balance. He asked Amitabh what do you know about this Dome and the material it is made of. This question was not suitable for this time but looking to his serious face, I thought it not to be worthless but carry more value. Thinking a while I said uncle I dont know about the material it is made of but from the beganing I felt that this dome is not made for this exhibition purpose, more beautifull easy structure could be made for this use. This Dome was made for some important purpose but at present it is used for touring exhibition.

Hearing me I saw after many days a satisfaction on his face and he said, well done my boy, we are sailing in the same boat so ther is nothng to hide. Your assumption was correct, this was not made for this purpose. Before Amerika's appolo mission to moon, russia made this to establish a Permanent Space station on moon but cancelled it for non availablity of water on Moon. Three of them were made in such a quality of fiber material that it can bear heaviest load and are weather and fire proof. This can be assembled by expert persons in eight hours and it has all the facilities for ventilation, against gas protection and proper electric lights for survey. Mir space station was made in the same way which ultimately increased friendship between Russia and Amerika ending the barier of cold war. Looking to the emergency it can not be taken back to russia so I have been told to sale or donate it as per my choice. With full heart I wish that the scientists and enginiers who have done so much trouble to make it, should not be wasted so If it is any help to you and you can use it to prtect youself, I will be too glad. You have talked about a fort for your shelter, I do not know how much it will be able to protect you but I am sure If you use this Dome properly, it definately will save you. I too have my selfishness. I am leaving Tanya and Juli with you, under, your protection, I too will try to come with family. If God helped us, in place of one, we will have two shelters that will save our life from coming disaster. What do you think of my offer, tell me? This unexpected God given gift made me speechless, This was not less than Karun's treasure. What was not in there. Electrice generator, air turbine, solar cooker, gas masks etc like hundreds of mateials I had not thought of any importance at the time of displaying it in exhibition. Each and every material was going to support in saving our lives against coming disaster. I and Raju both were looking at uncle with bewilderd eyes. Once again uncle repeated the same question about my deccision. My eyes fiild with humbleness, standing up I took hold of uncle's both hands and said uncle, who had the blessings of a saint like you, the evil itself can not harm him. Now I am prety sure that we will face this God striken disaster bravely and strongly to become successfull. Tanya and Juli too had a smile of hope in their face, Terishkov uncle without any delay typed the donation and authority letter and gave it to me saying, he is leaving Tanya and Juli in my protection as he has to go back to russia that night. I immediately phoned Gauri and told her in detail about the valueable gift of each and everything Terishkov uncle had given us. Hearing this Gauri became too glad and said Bhaiya second shelter of this kind will help us a lot in saving ourselves. One more thing I just remeber is that we should close ourselves in the shelter for ten, fifteen days to adjust ourselves in living there, so that if we feel anything short, we could arrange it in advance. These advance training will boost up our energy in combating obstecles which we are going to face in future. We can not repay our debts to uncle for this valuable help but we can repay some part of it by accmodating his family with us at the time of distress. We decided that to day Tanya and Juli will shift their luggage from hostel to the uncle's tent to live here. Till Jagdish and his friends come for dismentaling the dome, we will select and pack the material which were important to us. Rest we will get it done by Jagdish and his friends. We all will go to the airport to sea off Terishkov uncle and afterwords with all the materials, hiring four trucks, we will proceed for Rampur at our earliest. An urgent matter came into my mind that here Jagdish and his friends were available to dismantle the dome but in Rampur who will assemble it? The only way left was to train ourselves in helping dismanteling and getting a fare idea of what we have to do at Rampur. We have not eaten anything from morning so we all went to the canteen and between breakfast, I explained them about the problem which everbody gladly accepted to do. Raju went to hostel with Tanya and Juli to bring their luggage and I began to sort out and prepair the list. As the list of needed materials increased, my morale too began to rise, all the modern equipments and utensils, and gadgets were there which will be usefull in coming years of our survival in an alien world. The picture Gauri had decribed of the coming disaster, it would be very dificult to come alive out of that. It was like a prisoner locked in a dark room, you have facility of dining and toilet but you can not go out in open. For most of the people, they have to live like that for months or years. We are so much acostomed to the present living facilities that we can not imagine living without light, fan and easily available drinking water and this is going to happen shortly. Those who are fore sighted, will train themselve to live in limited resources. Most of it, will depand on Governments decisions, to educate the people about how to face the coming disaster, how to cope with them and how to be self sufficient.

The first priority in the list I had given to was, Electricity. There were four types of Electric genraters in the exhibition. First manualy oprated mechanical divice, a small genrater conected through two gears operated by hand or foot, second a household cabin fan type which can be used in great wind and third a conical shaped to fit on open space, fourth a long shaft which could be used in running water. Second priority was of long life lithium batteries which will collect the electricity generated. Third were different types of LED bulbs. As per my thinking in darkness we wont be able to survive for long. The use of candles and oil lentarn will last not long and to get constant supply of electicity we will have to use genretars. The list concluded to weather testing gadgets, gas masks, solar panels and cookers, water purifires, and chemicals, battery operated kitchen utensils, surjical instruments and so many other items that will be usefull in future. At four o clock Raju came back with two workers, I was surpraised to see Tanya and Juli in workers dress. Raju told me that Juli has suggested to dress themselves in working cloths to help in dismentaling so they have bought it in market with two extra set for Gauri and Manish. House hold dress were not fit for working. I understood that mentaly all were prepaired for the challange coming ahead. I had already completed the list so we brought boxes from outside in wheel barrow and noting the number started packing. By seven in the evening we had packed all materials in their box. Tanya and Juli were peraspiring but they never complained. I and Raju both were surprised for their zeal in working. Sfter washing ourselves when going to canteen for dinner, I congratulated them for heir help in packing, tears began to roll their eyes and they said these were of happyness, in a foreign country to get good friends like us, they were fortunate.

Next day at nine in the morning Jagdish with Jai and omprakash arrived as promised. I introduced them to Tanya and Juli. Between breakfast I explained them the orocedure we will adopt in dismentaling the Dome. At first we opened all electric wireing and curtains, than packed table, reks and floring. Raju with Jagdish started opening bolts by power

wrench and with the help of rope Jai and Om took out
outer chanels, then panels and at last inner chenals. Before
lunch working and helping togather we were successfull in
completeing half of the job. Realy it was wonderfull to look,
all working like robots. An hours rest for lunch, boosted our
energy and by six o clock, middle ring, observation post,
nine pillers and bottom ring, all were taken out and packed
in crates. Before saying boodby, I paid Jagdish, om and Jai
one days extra payment as bonus and thanked them for their
help in time. At noon uncle has already phoned that he was
leaving for Masco that night so we were expecting him any
time, As soon as we saw his car coming, we all ran towords
it. In between these days, his behaviour and intention to
help us all the way, had made a great impression on us.
Embracing Tanya and Juli he stood for some time, he looked
older than his ege. The deep sarrow he was feeling, we can
see on his face. He seemed to be in some doubts. He was
leaving his Tanya here but his younger daughter and wife
were waiting there at Russia for him. He shook hands with
me and Raju and said, well done my, now I know that Tanya
and Juli will be safe amongst you. Sipping cofee, sitting in
front of tent, he told us that he is leaving by nine o clock
flight and asked me if ant thing more I wanted to know. I
had only one question to ask which was ailing me, no time
was left so I asked uncle you have already told us about the
construction of Dome but pleas tell me for which use the
observation post was made? He smiled a little and said in an
unknown place like moon, it was made to observe around.
It has powerfull search lights on all four sides. In addition
it has exhast fans fitted inside the center poll to give fresh
air. It has some instruments to detect various gases and air
pressure. The two way control, are fitted on the post and

poll. The way to use them is written in Russian language so taking the help of Tanya, note it down and learn every body. Please note down my setelite phone number but use it in emergency only. The time of flght was near, so we all started for Airport. For Tanya time for separatio was approching fast so, she could not control her weeping, tears were rolling her eyes constantly. We were finding ourselves helpless, consoling Tanya in sothing words uncle too were unable to di anything. Before departing uncle again promised to come back soon and said fairwell to us. Juli was trying her best to console Tanya, she too started weeping. Tanya has only one word to say Papa, Papa.

CHAPTET 5

FROM RUSSIA WITH LOVE

YuriTerishkov

This had been my third day at Rajdut hotel when I was informed that the trucks containing exhibition material had reached at the ground to be unloded. My assistant Dimitriz.s ilness at Bombay had increased my responsibilities. I was unable to understand as to before the exhibition starts on 14th novembar, how the Dome will be assembled, who ill do it, whether it will be ready before the time or not. At present I had not been able to get the trucks unloaded. The contracter Ayangar & co. too was not responding to my call. This was my last working year and so for I had a good record of working but this year it seems, my reputation is at stake. I thought that the truck drivers will help me but they not only refused but are constantaly herasing me to unload the trucks before morning. Standing there I was looking for some one to help when I saw a young boy sitting beside teashop. Thinking he might help, I went to him with truck drivers. His personality, way of talking plus a badge of Bitco Corp. on his shirt pocket, insured me that if he agrees to my offer, my work will be done and it happend that way. He did not enquired about payment or any thing but going with me to the office, completed all formalities. I was surprised to look at his selfconfidence. I understud that this young man is more matured than his age and nothing is imposible for him. His name was Amitabh sharma. I had to see now whether my decision was correct or not. He passed his first testing, in geting the trucks unladed in the night as per my instructions. In the morning I called him through Tanya, at the hotel and showing the pictures, asked him if he can assemble the Exhibition Dome in ten days. He accepted the offer too. I thanked God for sending a dutifull young man to me at the time of distress. I became confident now that if I offerd him the post of Manager which my assistant did previously, he will accept it too. Tanya too vouched my proposal because we had no other option left. After that I and Tanya both began to relie on him very much. Tanya's friend Juli too was impressed by Amitabh. He never lacked anything. I began to think in mind if God could give me a groom like him for Tanya I will be too gratefull but it was not possible. One day Tanya told me about Amitabh's younger sister Gauri, who was asking Tanya about the reality of Russia's chenal elevan's programme about an Astroid. I was surprised to think that what Gauri has todo about Astroid and what she will do knowing all this. I did not give any importance to that. One day when I was talking to my Masko friend Dubraski by the way I asked him about chenal elevan's proramme about Astroid. He told me about a famous astrnomical scientist Velinkov, who had discoverd an Astroid which had saved itself from the clutches of Jupiter and moving towords Mars. With a little diference it could move to Earth and that will be too dangerous for us. All scientists are looking at it with great eagerness of coliation with Mars. This is going to be a great event after Hally's comets coliation with Jupiter. When I heard this I again was surprised about Gauri's enquiry but I told Tanya to tell Gauri about this information I got from Dubraski andbecame busy in my work. Only four days were left for the exhibition to end when Dubrasky's phone surprised and terrorised me. The same Astroid was moving towords Earth. Why the route of astroid changed, nobody could understand. It was defenite that the astroid was going to colide with Mars that is why all the scientists were consantrating on Mars but when the astroid did not reach Mars on probable date, than the scientists became horrified in confusion. All began to search the cause and when they found it, were shocked. Astroids size had lessend but it had changed its direction and was moving towords Earth. If the Astrois is not destroyed or not forced to change its direction than nobody could save earth from destrction. Accepting their responsibility two of the top scientists had comited sucide. It is possible that human species become extinct like dynosours. Dubraski had warned me to come at my earliest. I was shocked and could not understand, what to do. How could I save my younger daughter Lisa and wife, who were thousands of km away. The astroid was expected to strike on china Mangoliya border which was at thousand km distance from my village. Tanya was safe here but can not be left alone. How to shift, my family, to a long distance, from the distruction site, I could not determine. Tanya too was terror sticken and began to weep. What ever was going to happen, was going to effect all human beings. I was told to keep quite was declared to general public. Tanya knew this so I thought it better to tell Amitabh also who had helped me in difficult time and I was not going to get another time to repay his help. I told Amitabh in brief about the coming disaster. At first he was shocked in terror but in reply what he said, I felt a deep love for him. In straght words he asked me. to come and live in India with them with my family. He told me about a fort near his town Rampur where we all can survive safely. I was shocked in surprise to hear an unknon person asking me to help and live with them, when their life too was in danger. I felt a great gratitude for his mother and father who had borne a child like him. Once again I was over whemed when his younger sister Gauri told me in detail about the coming disaster and how to save us. I was terror stricken. I had not imagind about what dificulties we will be facing in future. I became glad talking to Gauri and when she too requested to come with family and live with them, tears rolled my eyes thinking, is it possible that both the brother and sister asking the same question. I could not think that in India, people have so much respect in their heart for foreigners. I decided that it was better for my family to accept their proposal. I gladly accepted the proposal. Tanya and Juli too agreed gladly. I had doubt in mind, without Governments permission, I could not leave the country, and if I told Tanya about it, she will not agree to stay here alone. Astroids severe destruction was going to be effect more near China, Mangoliya border and at Russia. At first the foreigners will be given priority to return home and after that to others. Easiest route will be by Air and millions will be waiting for that. We will not be getting any chance for that. I had only one way left and that was by road which was going to be dificult. I had one friend at Kajakistan who will help me going through Ujbekistan and Tajakistan to India by my big wheeled touring Bus. I have visited those places with my touring exhibition. In Tajakistan I had seen many big caves which might be suitable for our survival against terrible rains, storms and floods. If I became able to reach Himalyan ranges safely it would be a great achievement. IF I could arrange enough food, water electricity and other materials Gauri had told I have fair chanses in reaching India. As Gauri had said that if darkness prevailed for years it may invite Ice Age. And moving towords equater, it will be helpfull too. In any way I had to try hard in getting to India. I had worked in Siberiya for two years and know about terrible cold. To face that, I had purchased and prepaired a bus with full facilities for survival in killing cold, in which my wife and daughter still live in the village, will help me this time also in getting to India. My wife and daughter are trained in shooting, they are not afraid of wild animals but of hooligans only. God save us, we dont have to shoot people to save us. My thoughts were broken when next day Amitabh told me about Gauri's phone coming at nine in the morning. When I received a message from headquarter, to leave the entier Dome here or donate it some one, I thought it better to give this Dome to Amitabh. The kindness he had showed in keeping Tanya and Juli with him, I can repay him by this gesture only. I dont know that the Ramgadhi fort Amitabh was talking about wouldbe safe enough in saving them I did not know but I was sure that by which quality and enginiering this Dome was made, it could save them in any disaster. For coming dificulties, each and every material was usefull for them. And as per Gauri's sugestions, two shelters would be better than one. Morning at nine when Gauri phoned, leaving this Dome with Tanya and Juli in Amitabh's security, my decition was correct. As per Gauri's thinking, what ever mental terror she suffered was not useless. It was real. There is a saying that well start is half done. I was sure now that what ever time it takes I will come back to India definately. I explained everything to Amitabh about Dome, Tanya too was with him to assist. With heavy heart I said goodby to them at Delhi airport. I with my country man and scientists am leaving to Masko hoping that their hard labour and developed latest enginiering will give them protection and strength to face the on coming disaster to my son like Amitabh as a small gift. With a desire to come back I am taking Bida. God may give them strength to win over the coming disaster. My comng back to India, surely depand on God.

CHAPTER 6

DISASTER MANAGEMENT

Terishkov uncle's departure has made me and Raju sad along with Tanya and Juli. His kindness and oneness had impressd us very much. We had already arranged through Bagga transport for four sixteen wheelers trucks to Rampur. Coming back from airport the only thing left was to talk and inform Gauri. As if gauri was waiting for the phone, she immediately began to tell the quantity and the number of the materials he had collected, We have to buy milk powder, tetra packed milk and dry fruits in sufficient quantity. Her next demand surprised us. She told Raju to arrange two jungle knife, two matchets for clearing the jungle, pistal and gun for every body. Tanya and Juli were listening our conversation and were surprised to hear this demand, not only they stopped sobbing but dieverted their attention towords our conversation. Gauri said Bhaiya God save us from bad happenings, but if that happened, we will be throne back to Stone age, we are niether so strong nor so brave so these arms will boost our self confidence but will save us from wild animals. You think how I tanya and Juli will save ourselves in that condition. One by one Gauri talked with Raju, Tanya and Juli in getting us feeling good. Tanya forgetting her sadness supported Gauri's sugestions and began to say that her mother and sister are trained in shooting they dont fear any one. She further said that we will not get any further time to visit Delhi so they should buy every thing they could remember. We decided that next day we will purchase and collect all things before going to Rampur. Gauri's multipul qualities has impressed me too much, in the way she had utilised time and its importance was comandable. I thought one more thing that if in future, the decistion making we put on her shoulders, we will not face any dificulty. I rememberd a saying that a good soldier can not be a good comander. But a good comander can be a good soldier too. In bright lite if we see, we were doing the work of soldier, Gauri was the Comander. I decided finaly that at Rampur we all will do as Gauri wanted us to do. Till Gauri was talking withTanya and Juli I was busy thinking all this. I had two more responsibilities on my head. first was to save us from coming disaster and the second important one to marry Gauri with Manish. I did not want that my mother's last wish to be incomplete, so I told Raju to buy proper wedding dress for Gauri and Manish. I was not sure about the availablity of drinking water at Rampur so I had asked Raju to buy twenty litre mineral water containers and enough waterpouch for emergency. Loading all the four trucks with all the materials and sending them at eight in the night, we spent the night at a hotel and in the morning dressing up in Raju's jonga jeep started for Rampur.

Winter season was on and we had put light warm cloths, feeling great energy pushing us to face combat, To freshen our mood Raju had switched on the streo and singing joking we reached Rampur at two in the afternoon. Gauri and Manish were, at the door, waiting for us. Through exchanging photographs by computer, they recognised each other but seeing in front, were over whelmed. At first Gauri put a holy mark of rice and tamrin on their forehead, garlanded them and with a decorated plate used in worshipping, a diya candle burning in the middile circled around them welcomed Tanya and Juli tears of happyness began to roll their eyes. They had never seen and expected this type of Indian welcoming, They embraced Gauri kissing on cheeks. This side Manish was shading tears in happyness embracing me and Raju. The time of maryment passes very quickly. On the dining table Gauri had prepaired and decorated many food items. Gauri sitting between Tanya and Juli, Manish between me and Raju enjoyed our meals serving each other and remembering old days. For Tanya and Juli, this was, an exceptional, experience and were praising Gauri continiusly. When the decoration of Tent started on the cortyard I told Manish about Gauri's and Manish's marriage to be held that day. Raju has already arranged all this by mobile phone previously. At first Manish was adment at such a time but I made him understand, reminding mother's last wish. Embracing me he promised to take proper care of Gauri in future. Uptill now Tanya and Juli did not know about their engagement and the time has come to inform them too. By this time the three girls were busy in chitchating in the room and when they saw we three coming in the room, they suspected something but when I declared about previous engagement of Gauri with Manish and informed them for marriage ceremont taking place to day only, Tanya and Juli jumped in merriment, embracing and congratulating Gauri. Gauri wanted to object but seeing my eyes filled with tears, understood why I had taken that decision. I told them that next day morning the ceremony will take place and we have to go to the farm immediately, for unloading the trucks. It was five in the evening when we reached at the farm in Raju's jeep. Trucks had not reached so for, Manish showed me 10x30 basement with toilet, he had constucted with almiras on all sides and told me about Gauri's sugestion for this basement and its usefullness. I was surprised because this was a utility I had not ever imagined it. The Dome was to be constructed here only and the basement was an additional security. I embraced Manish saying he had done a very unique job and tell me what more you have done in my absence. Manish suggested us to come with him to the fort. Tanya and Juli has only heard of Ramgadhi fort but arriving there became astonished including me. He has changed the inside appearance completely. It looked renovated by repairing and white washing. Surveying all we congratulated Manish for his hard work. I began to believe that this fort is going to be a great help in saving us from the coming disaster. By this time all the trucks had arrived and so with the help of crane, which Manish had brought, began to unload the trucks beside the back side grain store. Manish was busy showing girls his farm. With in two hours all the crates and boxes were unloaded Manish served us home made milky tea. Leaving the assembaling for next day we returned back at eight in the night. With the help of Raju, I arranged every thing for marriage ceremony which was fixed at elevan in the morning. Tanya and Juli were in great spirit, as they were going to witness a novel ceremony. Gauri woke up at six in the morning as she had to do all worshiping arrangements. At first she prepaired Tanya and Juli by dressing them her Sari and blauze after words she too dressed herself in wedding dress. At exact nine in the morning Gauri and Manish siting side by side the worshiping was started by

Pandit ji. With full traditional way I did the Kanyadan by which the bride is handed over to groom in the presence of God. When the seven circles around holy fire were completed Tanya and Juli became emotional. They both were talking in Hindi, time to time they asked questions to understand the procedings. We all including guests enjoyed their queries. When, the last function of separation came, my eyes filld with tears. Gauri and Manish standing in front of mother's picture asked for blessings. The holy man Panditji completed both the functions of sepration and Manish's house entering with sanskrit shlokas and God blessing. By three o clock the guests too departed. Uptill now I had lived in Gujrat and at Delhi, alone but never felt lonelyness. Gauri too was in the adjoining house but feeling lonely and a bit tired I lied down on the bed closing my eyes. After a while I felt a touch of soft hand on my forehead, I opened my eyes and saw Gauri smiling and Tanya, juli, Manish and Raju laughing at the door. Gauri said Bhaiya I had promised mother that I will not leave you alone till you are married. You have already done as per your wish, now get ready, we have to go to farm, much work has to be done now. See we are dressed and ready to go. Realy they all were dressed in working cloths. I was filld with joy. Tanya said Amit ji to day is a good day, why not we worship and begine to start the Dome at Farm. what do you say? All agreed to her suggestion. Manish went to fetch Pandit ji on bike and we in jeep reached at the farm. To worship the ground, it was necesary to mark the circle, Raju opened the tool box and took out the rope with nails attached. He hamered the big nail in the center of the ground, strached the rope and moving in round, scratched two circles as equired. Calling the help, on east side a small portion was cleared of grass and painted with cowdung. Worshiping material s needed we have with us so, as soon as Pandit ji came, the worshiping started with sanskrit shlokas in traditional way, lightening scented sticks and offering sweets and flower etc he spread over the ground with sacred Ganges water. After this some work had to be started so with power grinder drum I and Raju moved it on the outer and middle circle. The helper cleaned the trench we have made. This was sufficient for the day. We had already decided that from now on Manish will live with us so after dinner, in one room Gauri with Tanya and Juli and in another room I, Manish and Raju spent the night. We had already planned that in the morning Gauri with Tanya and Juli will prepare the lunch at farm and take dinner at home. It had an advantage that Tanya and Juli will become familier with indian way of cooking. All the problems being solved in this easy way, all were pleased. At night washing ourselves we all gathered in mother's room to pray and worship. Tanya and Juli were watching all this very minutely perhaps thinking that if they had to live here in future they should know Indian tradition as well. From mornings celebration too much food was left hence enjoying it on the dinner table, we decided that each one will tell about the work they know well or intend to do. At first, Gauri said friends, as I assume that in future we have to live in darkness at least for six months or more, that depands on weather so we have to arrange electricity for twenty four hours a day. Gods grace and Terishkov uncle's help we got this Dome apart from fort, I suggest that we should live for fifteen days on each shelter to be accustomed in living there. If we felt some thing lacking, we will improve it. We have to finalise our daily routine. Daily Yoga, cleanliness, bathing, brearfast and work allotted, then rest. At evening, reading, music, tea, sports, left over work, dinner and rest. Two persons, for security watching, recording weather changes every fifteen minutes. if we see a sign of danger we have to inform every one. I think we should have some discusson and sugestions too. I will prepare food with the help of Tanya and Juli. Morning worshiping and exercise I will manage too. I said that I will install generaters in both the shelters and will manage battery charging. Manish said he will secure food products and supply. If he got space he will prepare nursery and try to grow vegetables. Raju said he will train every body in rope climbing and use of arms. Tanya said she will instruct them about electricity and any other work she was given. Juli said she will give first aid training and use of certain medicines. This work division made them stronger in belief that every body was usefull in certain field and will face the challange bravely. We congratulated each other and said good night for next days hard work.

Terishkov uncle had said that in expert hands this Dome can be assembled in sixteen hours, we were not experts but as I had already done it, I knew if done with a planning, it could be done in tenty four hours, so I divided the work by making pairs of I and Gauri, Manish with Raju and Tanya with Juli. Except the observation post, all parts were light in wait. Manish and Raju opened crate one, taking out outer beams, gave them to Tanya and Juli and I with Gauri fixed it in the place with the help of plastic hamer. This way we started the work of assembling the Dome. Gradualy the work became fast and in two hours we have fixed the outer ring. I had explained them to understand number and colour code printed on each part so with a little guidance, all work started smoothly. We made a trench for cross beam and fixed them in place. By the time girls were prepairing food we had fixd all the eight round poles in place. When we sat for lunch, I called the farm help Sonu and his wife to dine with us They became glad and dined with us happily. It is very rare in India, master and servant dining togather. Now we three were qurious to know, who made the vegetables tasting so good, Tanya and Juli looked hesitent but Gauri proudly declared that Tanya and Juli had made all the things, she only told them the method. We congratulated them for their first indian cooking. To pass the time we went to the fort, where Manish told us about his new discovery of finding a basement and an easier way to come out to the field. He said that when he was cleaning the floor with water, he saw water disappearing in a crack and when he lifted that stone, he saw stairs, and coming down he found the basement with toilet. Its back side was blocked by rubbles. When he got it cleared and came out, he was surpraised to find himself, out of the fort, near our fields. An easy way, to our farm. For security he had fixed a door there and locked it from inside. Manish further told me that he was facing a problem of filling the well with water, so I investigated and found conected to the well a sloping drain from outer wall ventilater from where a cold breeze was coming in. I looked thru the vent and saw below the big tank filled with water. The puzzle was solved, this was the older way of filling the well with leather bowl called Mashak. By rope they pulled the Mashak full of water upto the vent and at an angel dropped the water which through filld the well.. When I told Manish about it he blamed himself for not thinking it earlier. When Juli enquired about electricity I could not answer immediately but Tanya suggested that if we fix a fan generater in the ventilater it will solve the problem. I agreed to her suggestion and said to fix it in two three days. Coming back from the fort, we all joined togather to bring the observation post where it was to be hoisted. By pushing and moving round ultimately we brought it to the center. I bolted it with the big round pole, fixed its other end to the center ring hinge, and with the help of two ropes fastened to the post, got leverage by pulling ropes from two side poles, guiding step by step, we hoisted the observation post and tightened it with bolts. To enter into the post the ladder was fixed too. Now to fix middle ring, Tanya and Juli holding side ladders, Manish and Raju took hold, ring piece, climbed the ladder, stood on it and myself climbing the center ladder, tightened the beam on pole. This way with little manuvering by six o clock in the evening, we had completed most of the work which neede attention. I had not expected this much of work in a day. We were sure now that in two days we will finish the job.

Next morning, at first the outer beam was jamed to the ground by hammering all twelve pyloons into the rings of bottom beam. We took out all chenals from the crate and put them inside. One by one the chenals were pushed into the groove of bottom ring and another end tightened with bolts to middle beam. Raju hanging on middle beam wearing safty harness did all the tightening with power wrench. Then Manish too wearing safty harness, sitting on middile beam and Raju at observation post plate fitted the upper chenals. All seemed to be normal except for Tanya, who some times looked, absent minded because she had not received any phone call from her father. It was natural but we could not help her. After, lunch rest, to have enough light inside the Dome I fited two search lights inside and conected it from grain store main switch. Then we started fixing penals which rested above chenals. I and manish pushing and hamering the penals into the bottom beam groove, Raju bolted them on middle beam. We did not fit the last penal which had a three by five feet door with a circular ring on both sides because we had to move all the other materials inside the Dome after words.. To fix the upper penals wearing safty harness I too had to sit at the top plate and push the penal in plate's groove while Raju and Manish on middle beam bolted the penal. This way all the penals were fitted. After resting a while Raju and Manish wearing safty harness and hanging on rope began to fix upper portion of the chenal above penals and bolted them by power wrench. In the same way upper chenals were tightened and at last the upper portion of miiddle beam was bolted down. In the whole working, nobody complained but at a nudge the work was done. We all moved around the Dome, hand in hand feeling satisfaction but a doubt in mind wether this frail looking structure would be able to save us from coming disaster. At about eight in the night Terishkov uncle phoned. Tanya spoke to him in Russian for a long time. She looked unhappy and had tears in her eyes. After words she told us that her sister and mother are well but her father had no chance of getting air tickets. He was making plans to come by road which was dangerous looking to the present condition. She said that from that day on to please the God she too will worship HIM with Gauri Didi for welfare of her family.

Next day morning we conected all the irrigation pipes up to the drain ventilater and filled the fort well with water. Second job was to seal the bottom ring with cement so that in case of heavy floods the Dome will be dry inside and safe. Manish had enough of the building material left from previous work and I had learned the mason work at Bhilwada so we prepaired the mortor and filling it in wheel barows filled the bottom ring outer trench. By the time it was completed we three I Manish and Raju were perspiring. The girls were busy packing all food stuffs stored in the grain store other wise they might have objected doing this type of hard manual work. Now we have to make ready living quarters which will have to be comfortable because we did not know how much time we have to live there. Inside the dome at south side we readyed two tents, one for us and another for girls. We did not have any use of big crates so we opened all its flaps and made a third room for uncle Terishkov and his family. A little distance away, toilet and bathroom. Their outlet pipes were conected to the outer gas plant. We deposited all the small crates and boxes inside to open them when they were needed. We had already decided to shift our all belongings of home here next day. A box with a cross mark we had not opened in the exhibition at Delhi was still lying unopened so to enquire what was in it, we opened it and I jumped in surprise, It had a generater and six long life batteries with sets of transformers and conection board. I thought to generate electricity in both the shelter, I will use them to give twenty four hours light which would be most helpfull at this time. The gladness did not last long, when we were having tea sitting on the boxes beside Raju's jeep, an announcement shocked us. The announser was saying that United Nation has called an urgent meeting making compulsury to attend all nations immediately to discuss an important subject. The decisions will be declared afterwords to general public. It has only one meaning that the coliation of Astroid is going to be a reality soon. The option the scientists had was only one, either destroy the

Astroid or be destroyed. Our heart beat began to run faster, I felt a sensation in my body, the mind became alert reminding me for urgency. We had only one satisfaction that Gauri had visualised this disaster by Gods will and had prepaired us in advance to face the chalange bravely. With utmost thankfullness we will accept, what ever He intends to do. Consulting with Gauri and Manish I decided to transfer all our belongings of home including Manish's house, here in the morning. Secondly we will keep our cows and dogs in the fort cow shade and bike, cycles and Raju's jeep inside dome. Manish said that he will keep his tracter beside gas plant covering it sufficiently to save it from rains and flood. We all could not sleep well that night and woke up early. Freshning hurridely started packing, Gauri could not withheld her tears Tanya and Juli too had tears in their eyes, we had our remembarence of childhood and parents, with heavy heart, gradualy we loaded all the materials including fridge, tv, radio, books leaving nothing, from Mani's house grain prepairing Dhenki, Chakiya, Soopa and all other naterial including 500 Ltr water tank, pipes, wash basin, beds cloths etc. By ten in the morning in Raju's jeep with Tanya and Juli Gauri taking worshipping temple with her, reached at the farm. We followed in loded truck. When we were busy arranging all the material inside Dome, Gauri in east side direction cleaning the spot, sprinkling sacred Ganges water, put the temple and did her worshiping singing holy prayers with Tanya and July. She went to the fort and in the same way arranged a worshipping place which she had brought from Mani's house. Raju has gone back to his quarters at Jaipur to bring all his belongings. To facilitate proper living in fort we loded the bullock cart, tracter trolly with beds, table chairs, utensils and all other needy things and deposited them in the fort basement by new route discoverd by Manish. Gauri with her friends became busy in farm kitchen to prepare a heavy breakfast. With the help of Mani, I arranged all kitchen utilities above the basement, dining table, tv and radio beside center pole. East side we left vacant for exercise purpose. Cutting and spreading carpets in rooms we finished the job. Tanya and Juli had shown their expertise today, on making breakfast and in a while the dining table was filld with a variety of dishes bread, butter, tost, jam, bhajiya, poha, mixture and tea. We had alredy decided that there would be no lunch to day in stead heavy breakfast, to save time for other important work. Chitchating and talking about the pending work, we enjoyd the breakfast tastely. Uptill now we had conected the light from grain store but after some days it was going to be disconected for ever so Tanya opened a 8x12 inches secret cover in the round thick center pole, by number lock and showed me numberd switches and their function which were printed there in russian. Inside were two plus minus 24 volt wire terminals and two pipe ends. When I conected the terminals to two 12 volt batteries and as per instrction, switched on first four switches, the bulbs below the observation post began to glow, spreading light every where. Inside the round pole a dual purpose fan was fitted, switching on no. six, air began to come inside and no. seven air flow was out word. It was a wonderfull idea. When Gauri thanked Tanya for russian enginiers inovations, she became glad and said we russians were very much impressed by western world's development but by sending the Sputnik in the orbit first, we proved that if man makes up his mind he can do anything he wants. I am feeling very proud of my country man that this dome will help in saving our lives.

Gauri and Juli embraced Tanya, understanding that she had come out of the miseries she was feeling in absense of her parents. She further said to me, Amit ji we can not use generator inside, it will be harmfull, producing monoxide gas, we will have to use some other method to charge the batteries. We opened two boxes and took out all five items which were made for generating electricity. Tanya began to describe their use and rejected solar panel, cone shaped turbine and water flow turbine saying we can not use them, looking to our present need. solar panel and cone shaped turbine are used in safe favourable conditions, where they are not damaged. Looking to our present need the fan shaped turbine will be more usefull in fort where we will get heavy flow of air which will rotate the inside turbine to produce electricity. This is a miniature model of present Air turbines used every where. This too if fixed out side can be damaged by storms carrying flying objects. We will have to think some thing new to use this in fort. The best option for this place, manual turbine will be the best. Not only it will charge batteries but will give us a good exercise too. We all were listening very attentively, being a new sbject for every one but the thing that surprised us was Tanya speaking with full of energy without any hesitation. We all claped, to encourage, Tanya. Fixed in the ground, by moving the big wheel by hand or sitting on one end chair and padeling moved the wheel and turbine. I demonstrated its function because every body has to do it in future. As per consumption we will have to keep a record and use it accordingly. To supply water for drinking and toilet use I fitted the 500 ltr water tank on the heavy wooden box plateform we had made for this. We could not use tubewell without 230 volt electricty but Our tubewell had a handpump fitted in it and a cemented tank beside it so first we will have to fill the cemented tank with water by hand pump and than conecting a small water pump by pvc pipes we will fill the tank above wooden box. We had too many light bulbs, switches and wires in a box so as per requirement I fitted them in all the rooms, in kitchen, on dining table and in toilet.

Completing all this we felt relieved and thought thar if we had to live for long time, this valuable gift given by uncle Terishkov will safe guard us in every dificulty. Our next job was to prepare our fort shelter habitable. Every thing should be as good as, done in the dome itself. As Tanya had explained, the safe place for fitting the fan generator in the fort was the vent which we used for water filling in the tank, so by cutting and nailing the ply boards used in exhibition for displaying I made a long box which fitted on the drain and opened at the cortyard for air outlet, only thing left was front grill and shutter which Manish had orderd for making and was expecting next day. By eight in the night Raju came back bringing his lugage and other usefull things. He parked his jeep inside. Now we had three bycycles, one motorcycle, one jeep and a tractor for future needs. Raju reminded that in the morning he will purchase and stock 200 ltr of petrol, diezel and kerosine oil for further use and keep them buried out side for safty. Nobody thought about it so we all praised him.

Between dinner on the dining table, Gauri told us about the daily routine, we will follow after we have done complete packing, all the needy things in both the shelters. Gauri suggested that after toilet, an hours yoga by me, half an hours excersise by Juli. half hour bathing, half hours praying and worshiping then a light breakfast, which will be prepared by we three girls. Till lunch time Mani, Raju andAmit bhaiya will do the maintanance work needed, and we will prepare lunch in the mean time. In the afternoon, after reading, or resting, tea and in the evening, sports by Raju bhaiya. Before dinner, subject wise discussions and rest for the night. My intention is that everybody should make himself, so strong that he or she could face any dificulty in future. Our first priority will be at the time when disasterous effects reach us here and strike our shelter. Those will be the moments for us to watch and prepare ourselves. What I have read, when Astroid colides, its speed energy converts into a heat energy that spreads out at a speed of hundreds of km. burning all the things on its way. After that roaring storms and burning stones and debries will start falling, nobody knows how much time it will continue. After that heavy rains, lightening and floods will start. I have read in Holy books that the rains continued for eighteen days submerging every thing in water. There fore any two persons on vigilance duty will have to maintain record for every fifteen minutes. In alternate duty of four hours we will change. Maintaining record will help us in finding the pattern of increasing or decreasing changes. We ll agreed to Gauri's suggestions. From today we were to live in the dome. In one tent I, Mani and Raju in another Tanya, Juli and Gauri slept. One night light and exhast fan were on. In the morning Gauri Tanya and Mani complained of not sleeping well feeling sufocation. For the first time I had seen Gauri blaming herself and complaining. This was a serious problem and it meant there was no cross ventilation. In normal condition we use windows for that and there must be some solution already made which we had not discoverd. I suggested them all to search each penal and find anything new. Tanya and Mani found a three inch long dent on penal three, five, eight and elevan and when pushed aside a light breeze coming throgh. The problem solved after breakfast we started loading things of all kinds of food, cadles, torches gas sylander, bed, cloths, masqito net etc and arranged them there. Mani had brought the grill and shuter soI fixed the fan on vent oox and coverd it by grill and shuter in front, a liitle inside the vent. The fan began to move round, I conected it to the battery and switch bord. With in two hours I completed all wireing and fixing bulbs on selected points. For cow and dogs, Mani fixed a bamboo top over cows, filling it with foder, salt and raw sugar lump in a way they could eat easily without wasting it. For water, we filled all the eight stone pots which will be suficient for a month. We hoped that the God will help them too in hard times. In between two shelters we had enough food, water and other things plus electricity to last for five years and more but we needed God Blessing more than any thing.

Eightth December will be remembered in human history, if the history writers were saved, was going to be the indestructible impression, when it was declared that the discovery and prophecy made by russian scientist Yuri Dimitryz was going to be true and an Astroid named Dragon, coming from east side at a tremendous speed of seventy thousand km per hour, is moving towords the Earth. As per super computer calculation on 7th January night at eight twenty two, IST 46 degree akchhans and 102 degree deshans at Mangolia China border that monster Astroid named Dragon is expected to colide with Earth. All efforts are being made to divert its irection or destroy it. Devloped by latest technology new atomic weapons might be used in destroying that Dragon. By advansed country in space technology like Amerika, Russia and Europian Space

Agency are prepairing three bigest rockets loded with latest destructive bombs to destroy this Dragon named Astroid. After an hour again three more rockets loded with bombs will be sent to destroy the Dragon if some thing is left. Hundreds of scientists world over combining togather are trying to face this chalange. We are sure that we will succeed in our eforts. In Earth's history of millions of years in past, many times Earth had suffered these type of disasters. Dynosours like big animals became extint but hundreds of secies survived. From that time on we have been devloping in leaps and bounds. If we use our knowledge and efforts in a right direction, we would be able to save human species too. If we could not change this Dragon's direction or could not destroy it, there will be serious destructive implications. The whole Earth will be engulfed in darkness for six months to three years and we will have to face roaring storms, heavy rains, floods and land slides. In advance all the people of entire world are being informed that they should make their safty arrangements in time. You might have to face three types of these dificulties:- 1 - Extreme heat and storm 2 - Sevier rain and floods 3 - Hail storm and snowfall. To save yourself and your family scientists have suggested some important directions which, if followed strictly, we are sure, you may save your life.

1 - In high areas, storms will be more dangerous but in lower areas, floods, so if it is possible, you make two shelters making rooftop strong to bear the impact of falling debries. Unless important dont come out or change shelter untill the conditions improve.

2 - To save yourselves from heated shock wave, cover the rooftop with thick mud. Make underground

two room shelter in sloping area, where you are safe in floods. In one room arrange for your living and in another room store your food, water and other needy things plus modern gadgets to give twentyfour hours electricity.

3 - In first three days, keep yourselves hidden in a wall shelf to protect from falling debries damaging your rooftop. Keep handy food, water torch and other needy things in arms reach, to use in emergency.

4 - On any condition, do not come in out. Keep a map of surrounding area and about your neibours, use walky talky if possible.

5 - Arrange twenty four hour safty check. Use food and water in such a quantity, which is necessary. Use packed water or pouch, make a soakpit for toilet and cover it.

6 - For ventilation make small holes below rooftop and a watching point to access outer conditions. Remember this is a question of life and death so try to live inside the shelter for fifteen days before, so that you are acustomed to that living and you can arrange the things you feel lacking.

7 - If you have a car, keep it in a seprate underground chamber with tank full, to use when it is normal afterwords.

8 - Dont use fire inside. For light you can use car battery. To charge the battery, use manual battery charger which will give you, a good exercise.

9 - To pass the time, engage yourselves in Praying, worshipping, reading books, listening music and playing indoor games.

10 - To save yourself from hooligans keep arms handy, you may need it at present or in future. Keep good relations with your neibours and help them if you can.

11 - After rains, temprature will fall and exceed to hail storms and snowfall resulting to below zero so in noeth hemesphere make your rooftop in curved shape. Try to learn from your previous experience.

12 - If you have arranged and prepaired yorself for this type of calamities God will surely help you. After the disaster move to a safe place and collect needy things, found out side. Who were not fortunate, collect all their belongings, to use in future. Make a group of needy helpfull persons and start living welcoming what the God has provided for you.

In United Nations emergency meeting, this twelve point guidance programme was announced to educate and guide the general public. It was expected that all the governments will follow the proposed duties to facilitate general public.

1 - To save the general public living on sea shore, from enormous Tsunami waves, they should be requested to move their selves to live in new colonies made for tham, 300 hundred km. away from sea, with proper facilities of sanitation and supply of drinking water.

2 - From available resources, dome shaped structures should be maid with full facilities. A centralised tubewell and electric genrators should be used, giving respnsibilities for protecting them by military personel who will live there.

3 - Where, structures could not be made, in an opposite side slope, steel containers colony with full facilities, could be made giving commond to military personal.

4 - Per person @ of 300 grams of food grains per day properly safty packed for three years, should be given to every family in advance. Food distribution system should be properly arranged.

5 - A medical kit containg medicines of Diareya, vomiting, constipation, sleepness and first aid box should be provided for each family.

6 - Through Radio and TV all information should be relayed every day continuasly.

7 - The information regarding safe places for living should be announced prior to the disaster continiously.

8 - Private construction of, safe basement designes should be prepaired by experts and relayed continiously by TV.

9 - For help, use of whistle and distress signals, should be advertised.

10 - Train and bus facilities should be declared free of cost. Try to provide free electric and water facility for maximum time.

11 - At least for six months prepaire and distribute dry food to general public, making in factories.

12 - The use of dry fruits, jam, jely, biscuits, choklets, popkorn, noodles, chips, sugar based products, tetrapack milk etc should be encouraged for collection for general public.

13 - All the military forces and police personal should be paid in advance, food and other needy things in

sufficient quantity and posted in their home town or other places to maintain law and order strictly.

14 -An arrangement is being done to send a trained astronamer into the space by setelite who will start orbitting Earth for several months and by radio will give correct information of weather condition on earth and probable safe places for living in future, at regular time every day in computerised translated international five languages.

Not only we hope but we are sure that if all the foresaid instructions are followed strictly, a new morning will be waiting for you. God help you.

Thanks.

Holding our breath, sitting in front of tv we all were listening announcement by United Nations. What ever instructions were announced were comandable but it was doubtful in hundred million population, how much people will understand and follow the advice and instructions. On earth so many places are there, where mere necessities, are not available, they are to struggle for them, only God was able to help them. Gauri came to senses first and said bhaiya it has been a great blessing of God on us that time to time He had directed us in making prepairations in advance. We are most obilized for his blessings. Once again we must check our food and water supplies in both the shelters. Outer atmasphere will be full of dust and smoke so to get clean air, we should make proper arrangements. We get oxyzen from tree and plants. question is whether we can grow enough plants inside the Dome? The answer can be given by Mani only so he said we have enough plants growing in earthen pots and if we can arrange twelve our light inside dome, it can help. In space station scientists have been doing this type of experiments for years so we too can do it. This had two advantages, through bulbs light plants will inhale corbondieoxide and in return will give pure oxyzen secondly living in light all day long will help our living normal. There would be only one dificulty that we will have to charge the batteries many times. One by one, everybody will have to exercise by hand or foot in operating manual charger, we have aleady installed. Yoga in the morning and operating manual charger in day will keep us in good shape. When every body praised Manish for his suggestion he became glad and said that uptill now he was thinking that all of them are working but he himself was doing nothing but today he feels that he too is doing something important. I embraced manish and said Mani my brother, do not ever think like this. Ask Gauri, in future you to show your full ability, our survivel will solely depand on your ability. For how much days our stock of food will last after the disaster passes away. You will save us by producing crops in the field, we will be working with you as helper as nobody amongst us know about growing crops. In between these months, you will not only teach us what ever knowledge you have gained in agriculture college but doing practicals, every day, you will have to make us farmers. Like a primitive man we will have to learn every thing. What ever you need for future, you will have to do it now. Tell me what do you think? Manish looked surprised and said Bhaiya I had never thought about it in this way, I am thankfull to you, for reminding me of my responsibilities. I will have to collect all kinds of seeds in quantity. Going today with Raju I will collect all the things including some books and equipments that will be needed in future. Raju too apolised forgetting stock of petrol. digel and kerosine oil.

Gauri and Juli were busy in store keeping when I rememberd about the working of observation post. I asked Tanya to assist me in understanding it by translating Russian instructions. We both climbed up by ladder. This was the first ocassion that Tanya was so near to me alone. Day light was streaming in through thick glasses. Tanya lost her confidence and weeping embracing asked me repeatedly, about why her father was not coming early, she was too much worried for her mother and sister, how uncle could take care of them alone. What shall she do to help them. I could not answer her questions, simply I tried to console her in words saying Tanya, if you too were gone with him, tell me, how could you have helped him in the time of distress? He is so matured and experianced that he will surely manage his safty. Try to understand. How much he must have suffered in heart, leaving you here, God knows but he had only one thing in mind that at least you will be safe here. He had said about coming to India by road. So he must have some plan in his mind. Please have patience, rest assured that he will inform us soon. Now explain me, what is written here in Russian. At first she opened the windows shutter, a cool breeze began to flow inside, then she began to read the instructions printed on a box and translated it, in Hindi to me. It said one to five switches were for search lights, fitted on four sides and for inside light. Two switches for exhast fan fited in round pole, five switches for meters measuring air pressure, air speed and detecting corbon, sulphure and oxigen level in air. The permisable leval too were written there. I noted all this and coming down, when I told Gauri and others about it, they all congratulated Tanya. Gauri embraced Tanya, saying uncle had, helped us, a lot by giving this valuable gift and that too, we got it, because of you. Sitting at a place and geting so much information, in a second, will help us a lot in saving ourselves. We were talking all this, when Raju and Manish arrived, bringing petrol, diegel, kerosine which we stored outside, making holes. Manish had too many bags of seeds, plus plastic trays. They too congratulated Tanya. Hearing again and again herself being praised, Tanya began to smile, forgetting her miseries. When I sugested her, to explain every thing to all of them, she agreed and did the same, taking every body, to observation post. At tea time Raju began to tell about the effect, UN announcement had made, at Rampur. There was a rush of people in banks, in market, in grain shops every where. Rumours spreading like fire. Heavy trafic on roads and police were posted in every corner.

We thought ourselves lucky to make all arangements in time. Away from town, on day light there was no danger but at night we thought it better to start night vigilance, sitting at the observation post. We three man, in four hours rotation will start night duty, sitting in the observstion post. To pass the time we will take help of radio and books. Juli asked Manish, Mani bhaiya I could not understand why you have brought these plastic trays and what is the use of them in such a time? At first Mani looked confused then said Juli, you must have heard about international space station orbiting the earth and their planning to go to Mars in Future. To get a regular supply of food, they are experimenting various new methods and one of them is Hydrophonic by which, without any soil, in water trays by artificial light and chemical nutrients, they grow vegetables, and I too, am going to try that method, so that if we have to live inside this Dome for years, it will give support to our life. The statement made by Manish, once more shocked us, we were in an impression that this event will pass after some time and we would be happy, but it might not happen that way. Not only we but the whole population of millions, will face the shortage of food. It will take years for the earth soil to recover and grow new plants and by that time, who will survive? Gauri was listening Manish's statement very atentively, and moving forward, took his hands on her's and with emotions said, Mani, my childhood friend, till to day I thought that you only do, what ever is told to you but I was wrong, You want to do every thing but for want of time, you could not do it, today in front of all, I opolize to you for my little thinking and I feel proud of, geting such a husband like you. Tanya, Juli, Raju and I congratulated Manish for his novel experiments, he was going to do and we all promised to help, in conducting this. All began to feel that problems are a part of our life and if we are thoughtfull, the solution too comes out of them.

In the begning, for four days we all went outside in sun light to walk around but afterwards, Gauri stopped us going out and stictly folowed daily routine. Our waking up, toilet, Yoga, exercise, bathing, worshiping, breakfast, battery charging, lunch, rest, reading, sports and discussions, were all done in time. We all began to enjoy our routine which before felt lika a punishment. Eleventh day Gauri declared a Picknic day and said we are going to the Godess tempele above the Hill to worship, taking our lunch and enjoy there. We all agreed to her suggestion by clapeing for a change. At eight in the morning, we started climbing the hill taking worshiping materia, lunch and other things. This time, not doing as we did in past by racing, Gauri started singing holy songs and we repeated. Tanya and Juli too were trying their best in singing. Whatever religon you folow but your words show your iner feeling. By the time we reached at the temple, our eyes filled with tears in gratitude towards God. Dutyfuly we worshiped Godess and prayed for the safty of all living beings. Greenery on all sides and cool air began to fill our heart with joy or it was Godess blessings we felt light hearted, we all started playing games as if our childhood days, have come back. The game turned into touch and run game. On the hill top, open blue sky, a cool breeze flowing exhiliareted us, we began to feel like birds flying. Half an hour running and touching game exhasted us but the winer was Raju. His agileness surprised us. When Juli asked Raju from where did he get this energy? Raju directed his finger towards Gauri and said, inthese past days, daily fixed routine and exercise had chased away his lazyness, he had become acustomed to, and the credit goes to Gauri Didi. Though she is younger thanme but her will power is tremendous. Her hard dicipline, not only to me but to all, had made us strong and dutyfull. I salute to her. Gauri looked embraced but said Raju Bhaiya, I had done nothing new, I had done the same thing our Hindus traditions say, I only reminded them to you. I had to worship The Godess but I had two more duties to perform, for which I had come here with you all. Now Raju bhaiya, let me see your hand pack, you always go with. Tacking that she tool out all the things, bynaculer, big knife, torch, matchbox, water botel, ropes, rain coat, polythene, first aid box and many hooks and putting down on the ground, Gauri said, Raju bhaiya, we do not need anything here but you have brought them with you by habit. Is not it a good habit? If there is any emergency, these will help a lot.

A thought came into my mind that we are in a position that any time we have to run away, to save ourselves in hurry, so I want to have everybody with this backpack and we should make our habit to keep it with us ready, so in emergency we will not be a burden on others. Secondly we must have a helmet fitted with torch which miners use in mines, so that our hands will be free. Tanya and Juli are new to these surroundings. It would be better if we all go and look around for any suitable shelter in emergency afterwords. I think Mani will guide us better who knows the area very well. We will do the needfull at our earliest but let me say something more important. I and Manish are married togather but our relationship is like fast friends and I know very well that what ever happens, he will protect me in every condition. A woman without a man is incomplete. I think how nice it will be if Tanya and Juli too get protection and support at the time of coming emergency. My coming to Godess for blessings will be sucessfull. As I know that you all have already comited to help each other in life and looking to the time and emergency, this relationship should be strengthen by marriage. Amit bhaiya and Tanya, Raju bhaiya and Juli, please think over, I and Manish are waiting for your decision at Godess foot. God had already decided their destiny. Gauri's proposal surprised Amit too, Raju had already showen his inclination in marrying Juli on his first meeting with Juli but Amit, liking Tanya, had never expected that it is going to be true in future. Hesiteting a little Amit asked Tanya, if you want to marry me, will Terishkov uncle give his consent? Tanya's face became red in shyness, keeping her eyes down she said once dady had asked me about you and he was praising you. He wanted to know about my liking but I had not replied because I had never imagined that, going to be true. How did, Gauri didi knew my wish, I am unable to understand. I will be honoured if she accepts me. Her eyes began to fill with tears. Amit, for the first time in emotion, embraced her and damping her eyes said I had aleady promisd Gauri that whichever girl she will select, I will marry. Raju and Juli hand in hand were waiting for our decision. This unexpected gift had filled us with joy so we proceeded towards the Godess temple, where Gauri and Manish stood beside Godess statue, waiting to finalize the ceremony. Gauri and Manish smiling put a holy mark of chandan and turmerine, welcomed us. What happened next, that surprised us. Gauri took out four golden rings from her purse and Manish four flower garland, gave one each to us, This preparation meant that they had knowingly decided this in advance. We were over whelmed, Like obedient student, we worshipped, we wear rings to each other and garlanded. The last moment was heart pleasing. We all were feeling happy, eyes filled with tears of joy, embraced in each others arms. Gauri began to say, you might be thinking that how did I understood your feelings towords each other. I had aleady told Mani to watch all of your actions and activities and being an experienced person, he had done so very honestly. That is why I arranged all this. What is going to happen in future, no body knows but inwhat condition I was married, how did we met together, it looks as if God has already decided it in advance. It seems to me as if we are supplementing each other. By coordination we will be able to save us from coming disaster. In every step, we will have to face new challenges and whatever I am doing reflects that God is bewaring us that the coming disaster will not be a small one, we will be tasted in every difficulty and to come out victorious. To celebrate I with Tanya and

Juli have prepaired some good dishes, so come and receive God blessings in form of delicious food. Sitting under tree shade we enjoyed milk rice dryfruit made kheer, puri, paratha, papad, and other things. Radio was tuned on music and we remembered our childhood days, Raju began to tell stories of festival days and our enjoyment in various occasions, when suddenly the music stopped and special news bulletin started. Please stand by for an important news.. As per UN announcement on 8 th December, from Amerika, Russia and Europian space agency, three huge rockets loaded with destructive bombs have already been fired to destroy the asteroid Dregan, on 30 th December, which will destroy the Dregan in space as per Gods will. How much perfect our aim will be, we cannot tell now. In front of these rockets high resolution cameras are installed, who will send a live image of the destruction. This unique destructive incident will be relayed live which you can watch on TV. Behind this another three rockets will follow to finish the destruction complete. This too you can watch live. If God made us sucessfull in our efforts, it will be a great achievement for human species. Dragon's debries might fall on earth. Soviate Russia is launching a maned satellite on 31st December in space, which will orbit the earth for six months. Geri Kerishkov, an astronamer had given his services to navigate this satellite. He already had spent four months on international space station. Taking pictures of earth, he will inform us about earth condition and guide us to safe places on earth. This will be broadcasted in five computerized translated languages at fixed time, every hour. You will strictly follow the safety regulations, you have been told in advance Fot safety measures all the gates of water Dams have been opened to save us from floods. From 1ˢᵗ January all water supply, train and electricity will be stopped so you are requested to make arrangements in advance. All governments have already started distributing grains. You are reminded again to stock sufficient quantity of water. In the beganing, use readymade food for ten, twelve days. Living in basement, keeping safe your food, and cleanliness, start practicing now. Prepare a map of your surrounding area for safe place. After heat wave and storms rains and floods will attack so repair your shelter immediately. If your government has arranged for radio broadcasting, do take advantage of it. If you have been able to save yourselves from storms and floods your chances of survival will be increased. Any disobedience of safety will be life thretning for you so be alert. Till 30ᵗʰ December, strengthen your preparations. May God give you success. Thanks.

We were listening radio announcements, terror striken. The happiness and enjoyment, evouperated in a second. We could not belive that we are standing on a brink of disaster. Without uttering a single word, collecting our belongings, saluting the Godess again, came down the hill and sat down on jeep. We rememberd, how urgent it was to look for a safe place. Half an hour distance a colony was being constructed, there only one house was complete and others were half done. The colony was at Delhi Ahmadabad highway. A second road went towards M.P. and on wards Luni river. All the area was covered with Babul trees. Searching around for one hour, we could not find any suitable safe place so went back to the farm. We have become accustomed in living in the Dome for ten days so next day morning, after bathing and breakfast, kept our manual charger and batteries in the basement for safe keeping and mooved to the Ramgadhi fort. Being at a height, atmosphere was pleasant. From window and ventilater in the front round room, light and air was sufficient. All felt that living in fort will be much better than the Dome. Gauri, Tanya and Juli became busy in arranging store and making lunch. I started fixing fan turbine in the vent and connected it to the battery. A speedy breeze moved the fan blade and bulbs began to glow. The shutter fixed on the turbine could be adjusted as required at the time of storms. By one pm all arrangements were done. We had three gas sylanders for cooking food, enough water in the well, and to save us from darkness, electricity from fan turbine. Behind backside wall Manish had arranged enough fodder and water for the cows. Gauri had decided to keep dogs with us, understanding their ability in sensing danger beforehand. The working space, compared to Dome, was less but enough as per needs. The underground basement discovered by Manish, was a great help. In an emergency we could move inside there and save us. We stored and arranged all the things in basement to be safe, if we had to leave this fort in future. We assembled in the front room where Gauri had kept the temple and stated our worshiping and prayers. Some days of singing had made Tanya and Juli, perfect in singing and when it is connected with devotion than it does miracles. We forget everything only nearness with the Almighty. Today we had the same feeling. Whatever happens to us or where ever we had to go, we will not be alone. In turn, we all did the lamp circling to the God and accepted the offerings of coconut powder and sugar.

After lunch, we climbed to the top of the fort and sat down in seprate corners. The effect of coming disaster could be seen in our actions. Everybody seemed to be lost in thoughts, trying to hide their fear. Suddenly a flute singing broke the silence. We saw Manish tuning his favourite song Aaja tujhko pukare mere geet re, mere mitva and Gauri looking at him with deep emotions and eyes filling with tears. Raju, Juli, Tanya and Amitabh all rushed towards them and embracing each other, like they did before at Kutubminar, they kept their hands on each others and Raju began to sing a song, Humko man ki shakti dena, a devotional song that inspired them, to do their duty honestly, doing wrong to no one. The song did a miracle, again they became joyfull feeling new strength and energy. The old routine started again. There was only one change, Gauri started Yoga in the evening too in stead of manual charging which was not needed here. We closed ourselves inside the fort. We began to look for anything that needed attention and attended it. Juli directed our attention towards ventiletars closing and Raju about the safe way, if we were forced to go to the Dome in darkness. Both were important. We closed all the ventilaters by stones and cement so that afterwards they can be opened again. The problem was how to reach from fort basement to the dome. In darkness, and heavy rains, it would be more difficult and dangerous to go outside. Raju solved it. He tightened his trecking ropes between basement outside door, to the dome entrance and wearing harness hooked it to the rope and trained everyone to go towards dome running beside the field up to the dome in darkness. At night Raju gave practice to ever one till he was satisfied. I had to congratulate him for this novel idea which I could not think, if tried too. With a helmet torch, running alone and then in pairs all became successful in completing this merathan run. In difficulties, cooperation and unity makes successful. Every day and night seemed hard to pass. All were worried and waiting for the coming space event of 30th December which will be remeberd in centuries to come, on which human existence was in stack.

CHAPTER 7

ACTION AND REACTION

The day of 30th December was like other days of the month with only one difference that it reminded the evil happening, which was going to take olace that say. The silence it criated had perhaps fritened all the creatures living around. It is believed that they know about it in advance and so had hide themselves in their nests. All over the world, people sitting in front of TV were trying to sustain their heart beating. In all announcement onlt one topic was being discussed. They were trying to describe their views in different ways. By computer animation the destruction it will make, was being drametised. The length and width of that Astroid named Dragon had already been calculated by the scientists but what is inside that seven km long monster Dragon and how much damage or pieces, the rockets loaded with powerful bomb would make, by its impact or which direction it will move to was, impossible to tell. When the huge rockets speeding at 30000 km, per hour will collide with the Dragon moving at a terrible speed of 70000 km per hour, what will happen, nobody could imagine. There was a theory that this coliation will make thousands of pieces of that Dragon and the problem will be solved but another theory declares that in the zero gravity of space the gravitational force of the Dragon will unite them again as one and will proceed on its way.

At 12 AM in the morning, the three camras fitted on rockets started showing rockets advancing in space. The Dragon was at the distance of ten million thirty five thousand km away looked like a tiny spot looked through telescopes. The modern technology has made man sucessful in controlling them in long distances too. All over the world, expert scientists, holding their breath, were busy directing the rockets. The future of human species was in stack. From a pin point, the size of Dragon was increasing minute by minute, the heart beat of on lookers too became fast. The tv clock had come down from hours to minets. One revolving demon orbiting in universe, traveling trillions of km, creating havoc everywhere, was coming to destroy our green pasture called Earth. First reaction from the public was, negative because, in computerised animation, we had seen many a times, various films, but this time, it was going to be real, not imaginatio that, man had made a source of entertainment. It was ging to be decided in minits, whether human species will survive or become extinct like dynosours in past. What the almighty God has decided for us was going to be known very soon. The rocket cameras were showing it from different angales. Each posibility was being discussed. All depanded on their formation, they were made off. If tha Dragon was made of iron metal objects, which was more likely, because it had traveled millions of km without being stopped or destroyed, it was going to wipe out, all of us from the earth. The dragon which had alraedy saved itself from Jupiter's gravity then if its one piece will collide with earth, it will do enormous destruction every where. To avoid their becoming united again by their gravity, scientists had fired three more rockets, loaded with destructive bombs, to finish them in space and we were going to watch them being destructed, live in our tv screen.

In 21st century, man has become soccessfull in understanding nature through their inventions but has not conquered it. Robing and looting incidents were happening, all over the world. To occupy safe shelter, to collect enough food, the hooligans were out of bond. Police and army personal were trying hard to maintain law and order but it was not enough. The roll of media was very admirable. How to make a safe shelter? How to arange things inside? How to signal distress? In all subject, they had invited experts to explain safe measures to general public. What they should do and what not, was discussed widely. Every minor thing was told again and again to save them from storms, rain and floods. To make them understand the precautionary measures, they had prepared a plan in percentage, to give them morale strength, if they are going to survive. as:-

1 - If you are alive after 48 hours – 10%
2 - If yoy are safe in seven days – 25%
3 - If you are alive after 30 days – 40%
4 - If you are still safe after six months 51%

If you had followed safty measures and instructions strictly for six months, then only you might be able to save yourselves, otherwise not. After that if you are successfull in getting safe drinking water, in saving, collecting and growing food, in getiing support from others, you will be able, in giving your valueable support in making a new world, in saving human species.

The ateroid Dragon was moing towords earth at an enormous speed of seventy thousand km, per hour. Before its speed was hundred thousand km p.h that had saved it in submerging in Jupiter but when it collided in asteroid belt with another asteroid circling there, not only it was divided in two pieces but the impact made it slower in speed of seventy thousand km.p.h.. One piece went away to universe direction but another piece was forced to change direction and that too, to towords earth. Scientists were following the same source of action, by computerized calculations, again and again, depanding on it, in changing its direction again by impact through bomb loaded rockets. Before landing on moon, they had practiced many times, by computer calculations and they were successfull in landing astronauts on moon. But when the future of mankind was at stake, they were going to exercise their whole expertise on this first and lost attempt. Hally comets impact with Jupiter was unique. It was believed that comets are not solide but made of water and snowdust but when it was divided in many pieces by Jupiter's gravity, and the the result of inpact it made on Jupiter. The cause of that much destruction it made, is still unknown to the scientists. The fear, that this asteroid Dragan is solid in mass had frightened them all and are more worried. The asteroid impact on Mexican peninsula had engulfed the whole earth in darkness for years. Will that happen again, nobody knows. These were the questions, which everybody wanted to know but were helpless. Only he will win who has the biessings of Almighty God, who had created this universe. Is the God sentencing us for the crimes we had done in the past in ilumanating thousands of species from green pasture of land calld Earth, for our comforts, or by droping atom bombs on Hiroshima and Nagasaki, killing hundreds of thousands innocend children, men and women, or by arranging arms race between poor contries in killing thousands of people in hunger and femine, or making clone had challenged God for his existence or the time unknown, these happenings are a game He always play.

Gradualy the Dragon was approaching nearer and nearer. It was plained that when the center rocket will dash with the Dragon, the two side rockets at a distance of two km will be ignited after a second automaticly, to get proper destruction force, to destroy the Dragon. This all depandes, at the position of the Dragon. If it was in a width position the chances of being a success were 51% otherwise anything could happen. Apart from this, below five thousand km, two more rockets with camras, at a distance of five km, were following to record the first impact. If the first attempt failed to destroy the Dragon, then these two rockets loaded with destructive bombs will be directed and detonated by the signal given from the earth control. Within seconds, this all was going to happen. Holding there breadth, all the scientists and people world over were waiting. The counting began ten, nine, eight, seven, six, five, four, three, two, one and with a flash, an explostion and the tv screen became dark for some seconds but what we saw, after words shocked us to bone. At the last moment theDragon has changed its position. The center rocket had divided this Dragon in three pieces on impact. One piece had gone away to other side but the second rocket blast had made the left over two pieces in a single line spreading dust and small pieces, advancing towords earth. An imaginary orbit line was made by computers to signify the actual happenings in space. It was to be seen whether these two pieces will be united by their gravity, whether our scientist's will be successful in their second attempt to eliminate the danger. A partic disturbance prevailed in whole of the world. People began to pray God every where, in temples, churches, masques, in the streets crying for help.

In Ramgadhi fort, we saw the first attempt to destroy the Dragon, being failed and our faces became white in fear. Perhaps the God was angry with human beings, otherwise first attempt would have been a success. The computers were instigating that both the Dragon pieces were advancing to unite. The speed had lowerd a bit but we were not out of danger. Ignorance is better than knowledge. Some people were not shaken. Thinking whatever happens to others will happen to them, then why to doubt in God's will. But if you know more you suffer more. The saying was tormenting us. Gauri has been suffering since long and has developed ways to save us. We knew about it only some days back. It was Gauri's strict regulations that she kept us busy all the time. By yoga and excercises we felt hungry and slept well. These two were enough in increasing our morale. Mentaly we were prepared to accept and face the chalange of disaster. Backward counting started. The rocket cameras were focused on the remaining two pieces. Missile technology was going to be tested. The scientists had to decide about the way these two rockets will attack, which piece. The medium were scientists but actually it was directed by God himself and it happened that way. On moving Dragon pieces, effective attack could not be done. Only a little time was left to calculate, what was going to happen to all of us, in future. Between hope and disappointment, it was announced that we have not been successful in destroying the Dragon or divert its direction and on seventh januvery at eight twenty five, as per Indian standard time, Dragon's three km wide big portion is going to strike at China Mangoliya border near Gobi desert and second smaller portion of one and half km after six minute at Atlantik ocean. This new development increased the terror. At present the only terror was of tremendous heat wave and terrible storms but now the tsunami waves will ingulf sea side cities, where millions of people live. Its heat energy converted into vapour energy, combined, how much more suffering they will give to mankind, nobody could imagine. It would be imposible to survive. Asuming this type of probability, sea side cities had alredy been warned and vacated but nobody had expected that the tsunami waves could effect upto three hundred km and more. This had shaken the governments. Only seven days were left. All the islands were going to submerge into the sea. At all corners of the Atlantik ocen, isunami waves were going to attack. UN has appealed to all people of the world to make all arrangements to save themselves and maintain peace and harmony. Try to follow the guidelines strictly. May God help you all. Thanks.

In reaction our faces became white. The pictures of destruction seen in computer animation began to come in our mind, terrible happenings, fire storms, people running hither and thider to save their lives, big trees and objects flying in the air, terrible heavy rains, big tsunami waves, floods these all began to remind us like films. Before our fear exceed more Gauri immediately took control in her hands, she switched off the tv. She reminded us that still seven days time is left and the scientists are not going to sit idle. It will take some time to enalise and come to any conclution for them but it is sure now by this last warning that the disaster is not for away. We should not waste any time and should be busy doing the work, we had been doing. For the last time, we should check each and everything because ther will be no other time. Come, we all should go to God for his kind blessings. One thing is sure that whatever man make development, many new inventions, ultimately that will happen, which the God had decided, at the time of creating universe. In the last century, many old civilization have been discovered, which were lakhs of years old and facts were found that they were lost suddenly. The reason beings, earthquakes, volcanic eruptions, tsunami waves and unforeseen asteroid impacts. More than hundred fifty craters were discovered which were made by asteroids. Thousands of people lived there but only those were safe, which were at the right place on the right time and by Gods will, had done their preparetions effectively. We have to see and judge ourselves that have we too had made eforts like them. Have we been doing all the things as directed by God time to time? These thoughts were disturbing our mind again and again, so we all standing on our knees, in front of small temple, were praying with deep imotions. Gauri's sweet voice resounding fort walls, gave an impression that we were standing on zero and seeing Gods big image in front. Sweet odour of smellingstick spreading all sides Gauri singing – Shantakaram bhujagshaynam padmnabham suresham,

We all were finding ourselves lost in His Praise. Since primitive time when men came into existence, at the time of distress, raising hands upwords, unknowingly praising God for benovelance. And he gained his blessings too. He may be of any cast or creed, he got peace. We all do the same. Is not it a unique thing? Everybody knows that the body is mortal but the feeling of oneness force him, in doing upliftment for human beings. All the living creatures, directed by unknown strength, spend their life livingly. We too were doing the same thing. Gauri completed her prayers. For a time we all stood in mock silence in prayers then we became busy doing our work.

Tanya and Juli had adopted the daily routine very skillfully and we were glad for that. We had not received any news of Terishkov uncle. Whenever we saw Tanya looking some where else, I felt sarrow for her. I wanted to contect him through satellite phone but his warning that he himself will contect us, stopped me. I reminded Tanya that he is safe and will contect us, when he reaches any safe place, gave her some assurance. Only seven days were left and in checking we found everything in order. Tanya suggested to see our previous recording of the disaster once more, to compare our preparetions if we had forgotten something. We all agreed and she started the laptop. After Delhi's demonstration, we could not dare to see it again. Who would like to see himself suffering that way again but the time had come to examine the truth of it. The scene of asteroid impact was beyond expectations. At a terrible speed, a huge shrieking fireball, creating many km wide deep ditch on earth, projecting huge burning stones high in the sky, fast speeding heated shockwave, falling burning stones on villages, cities and people running crying to save their lives. Seeing all this Gauri stopped the laptop. Frightened we all stood up. The deep impact, creating havoc and destruction, thousands of km away, crossing Himalyan ranges, the fireballs would reach us and destroy everything, made us thinking and that frieghtened us. We could not believe it but what we saw, fireballs falling all over tha world, made our mind to accept that it was a reality. Would that Dome be safe enough to protect us from, Firenado. The fort made of stones will be safe but what about the dome. Gauri started saying, bhaiya, Terishkov uncle knew everything and had said that this dome is strong enough to bear heat and heavy impact so we will be safe against fire but the surrounding area of trees will burnt down. This will rise temperature and heavy smoke will suffocate us. I can think only one solution that forest people apply. In time they cut all trees and vegetation before the fire starts. The question is whether we too can do it? Mani himself can answer this question. Manish did not reply immediately but thinking a while said, Whatever Gauri had said is true but it is like destroying your own garden. For this we have to cut every single tree and vegetation, which took too much time and labour but nuthing is more valuable than life. For house making I had already cut some trees, we will bury them and others we will cut tomarrow, putting them under ground. They will be usefull for cooking afterwords. If we survive, we will make our garden more beautiful. From tomarrow morning if we start cutting, it will be a good exercise for us and to save the wood, we will bury them under ground or dip them in tank. They will be usefull for cooking in future. To save ourselves from burning flames, we could not do anything more. Second problem of heavy rains and flood, we were helpless and fully depanded on God. It was a reality that more heat brings more rain. The Dragon's enormous speed energy was going to be converted in heat energy and falling fireball stones all over the world will burn all the forests, which will increase the temperature so much that all the water in land will evoparate, making heavy clouds that will rain how many days, nobody knows. That rain will submerge most of the land, we have been listening and reading in holy books. They are described as Pralay.

There was only one thing in our favour that our farm was ten feet higher and the sloping road after three km meets the Luniriver. Our security, depands, on the quantity and duration of the rain. Except praying to God, we could not do anything. Next day morning, after breakfast, we gather, inside the Dome. At first we checked each and everything minutely then taking cutting and cleaning tools started the work outside dome. Taking the help of air direction we burnt all vegetation gradually. Cut all trees and pressd it underground. By the evening we were standing on a burnt field. Deep anguish had made us speechless. Silently we came inside the tent, questioning ourselves whether our green pasture of land, our earth will look like these, afterwords. The shadow of terror was so immense that nobody touched lunch. Unable to understand, what to do next, everybody was hiding eyes and were sitting silently. Gauri too who had been a symbol of hope and dedication, today was feeling helplessness in finding a way to overcome this terror sticken feeling. Tears began to roll from her eyes. For the first time we all saw tears in Gauri's eyes. Immediately we gatherd, around her. Tanya took Gauri's both hands on her and emotionally said Didi, till today, we all were taking courage from you, and by the grace of God, and will be in, future also. I have full faith on you. Why are you worring so much? Everybody is near with you. Look at me, papa, mummi, younger sister, nobody is with me here. What has happened to you that you have tears in your eyes? Gauri embraced Tanya and said Tanya, all of a sudden I rememberd that life is so perishing. What is today, may not be tomarrow. Since childhood I imagined some dreams. I thought that when Amit bhaiya will get married, there will be great rejoicing, a newly wed bride will come as

Bhabhi. We will enjoy everything but God has not accepted my wish. These thoughts bring tears in my eyes. I selected you to be my Bhabhi but could not welcome you as wanted. Now tell me, from today, if I call you Bhabhi, you will not mind? Tanya began to say Didi, you are older than me, you may call me whatever you like but what is this Bhabhi word, I could not understand. Smiling a little Gauri explained, we call elder brother's wife as Bhabhi. Amit bhaiya and Raju bhaiya both are olderthan me so I will call their wife Bhabhi and this way, you and Juli both are my Bhabhi. Hearing these words Tanya and Juli both pleasantly embraced Gauri. Tention, evouprated instantly. We were inside the Dome so Gauri suggested to check everything, generator, battery, lights, drinking water etc. once again and locking the gate we went back to the fort before it became dark.

All the three girls became busy in kitchen and we switched on the radio to hear some latest news. Previous instructions were being repeated again and again. Full days hard work and tention had tired us, so after dinner we went to bed early. In our daily routine, a little change had been done. Yoga and exercise were to be done on fort top terrace in sun shine, as suggested by Tanya. Vitamin D give strength to our bone and that too we get from the sunlight. Nobody knew what is going to happen in future and when we will be able to worship Sun again, so everybody welcomed the suggestion. The practice of night running with backpeck, from fort to dome, looking after tha vegitables grown by Manish at dome, generating electricity by hand or foot, rope exercise by Raju, became our daily routine. We all were longing for only one thing and that was happiness and enjoyment which had gone missing. We wanted to but could not laugh. We only felt at ease when worshiping, praying. It became a daily routine in morning and evening. Tanya and Juli too prayed dutifully. When all three girls sang together in their sweet voice. We became over whelmed. Suddenly the radio announcement stopped, increasing our heart beat. At first we thought radio had some problem but it was o.k. Doubt became illdoubt. Wether astroid impact happened before time. We had to console ourselves that computer calculations can not go wrong. We were worried enough but thought it to be known next day. Suddenly satellite phone started ringing. All were astonished. Since long, we were waiting for its sweet tune. Tanya hand trembaling with emotions, started speaking saying Papa, uncle replied, yes Tanya I am speaking, with very difficulty, the conectio has been made. I have reached karakoram, got a safe place too. Do not worry, mother, Lisa well, talk. The phone was disconnected. Tanya in gladness began to weep and said papa, mommy and Lisa are safe now how much the disaster will be, w will meet someday. We congratulated Tanya for her family being in a safe place, getting away thousands of km from destruction site at china border. Juli too was over whelmed and began kissing Tanya again and again. This happy news filled us with hope and energy. We became sure now that whatever comes ahead, we will face the chalange and cross it.

CHAPTER 8

DOOMS DAY

In the morning, after taking bath, on the top of fort terrace we were worshipping Sun God. After offering water and flowers to Sun God and all the four directions, we closed the door tightly and came down in the front room, where Gauri had installed the Temple. Today we worshipped in pairs. Gauri with Mani started the traditional worshiping by offering water, rice, flowers, sweets to God, then Amit and Tanya and last Raju and Juli did the worshiping. In the end we all stood up and singing prayers in Sanskrit, mooved around the Arti by lighting fire lamp, around God and four directions. After this, we stood in silence for two minutes praying God to give peace and courage to all human beings and living things. We had closed all doors, windows and ventilaters tightly. All lights were on. Smelling sticks were lighted in all rooms. The good news came when radio announcement started again, which were closed since morning. The comentater was informing us that to connect with Geri Kerishkov, who was circleing the earth in satellite, the transmission was closed. An arrangement has been made to relay news, every two hours for fifteen minutes, by Geri Kerishkov. Russia had sent a satellite in space to give live cocerage of happenings on earth in computerized translation of five international languages. At a fixed time, every two hours, for fifteen minutes, live coverage will be given by Geri Kerishkov from the satellite. He will inform you about the destruction made by Dragon on earth. For safty of people, he will describe weather condition, cyclones, tsunami waves and all the things. Please listen to him and do accordingly. This was a great achievement for the people. You will not feel yourself alone in the world. Somebody is looking at you and guiding you to avail safty.

We heard Gery speaking. I am Geri Kerishkov from Russia and giving you the latest news about weather conditions on earth from the Russian satellite, five hundred km above the ground. At present I see half of the earth in darkness of night and half ligted by sun. I am not a scientist but an ordinary man like you. I have no family but in the time of distress I heve decided to give my services to the world, understanding that I too have the same geens as you have and it connects me to you as my family. I can not do anything now but afterwords I will guide you to safe places, give information about the weather, cyclones, rains and floods. It will only be possible, when the conditions improve a little. Do not take chance, sit tightly in your shelter and hope the God is with you to help.

Eagerly we were listening Geri speak. The time of impact was coming nearer and the brain started supplying adreline to the body. That is done automaticly, at the time of distress or emergency. We began to feel sensation in our body. Coming forty eight hours were going to decide our fate in this world. What ever guidelines and instructions were announced by UN, were going to be tested now. We too have decided the division of work and were following strictly. In primitive days man looked at these asteroid and comet, surprisingly, knowing nothing about them but his trong will to survive and quriacity had made him, the most powerfull among species. We had switch on the DVD player with religious songs. Raju was at the moniter screen, visualizing outside, through cc camra and noting temperature and air speed. Rise in temperature and increasing speed of air will warn us against coming disaster, Every governments had made concrete bunkers for media personal, where devoted man and women will be guideing general public for safty by regular radio broadcasting. This impact was gong to change weather pattern altogather so in future our present record will help a lot. In pairs of two for four hours, we started our daily routine, maintaining records of weather. Daily ration of dry fruits and water pouch we kept near us. Minutes advanced to the hour gradually approching eight in the night.

Holding our breath, we were sitting in front of tv for live telecast of twenty five minutes by Geri Terishkov from the satellite, In controlled voice he began to speak. At this time, I am traveling at the height of thousand km, parelal to ground above Tibetan plateu. The whole world is in darkness. Still the Dragon is forty thousand km away, looking like a dot. At about four hundred kmabove in earth's outer atmosphere, we will be able to see both heated asteroids seprately. Their friction with air will start in the form of burning trail, which could be seen in naked eyes and within two three seconds the big asteroid piece will hit the earth. After five seconds another asteroid piece will hit the Atlantic ocean. From first impact, I will try to follow the second astroid. It all depands, on the result of first impact. The smoke and burning stones will be thrown out in the sky beyond limit. To save myself, I will have to be carefull and will go upwords. The impact may stop our relay for some time, so wait for some time. When the weather clear, I will try to guide you and think myself fortunate in helping you. The survival in those conditions will be too much difficult. I will try my best to navigate you to safe places, where living will be easier. Please wait a second, I have seen the Dragon, they are approaching fast, it looks it had gained more speed, here now they had enterd the outer inospere, burning hot, spreading tail and ilumnating white light more than the sun, oh God, save all humanbeings, I can hear its roar even in my closed cabin, what it would be outside I can not imagine. Night sky of the eastern earth looks as if detonated by lightening itself. Oh god, oh God, it is going to hit and I have never imagined, so many atom bombs ignited at a time, a huge colum of smoke with burning stones rising to the sky, like supervolcano iruption, shochwave spreading like a…oh the smaller dragon is going to hit the Atlantik ocean and and oh, I see a huge immense wall of water rising to th sky,.. suddenly the transmission went dead.

Till now, sitting in front of tv, we were watching our own destruction live, which ended suddenly., Warning us that anytime the shockwave may hit us. WE had already seen the Dragan's death march. Felt the earth trembling in terror, seen the smoke and burning stones reaching the sky, seen the darknight torned into daylight. Those will be fortunate who died at the first impact, remaining people will suffer how much, for how many days only God knows but it is definite that it is not going to be easy. The sufferings born by him since stoneage of hunger, thirst, heat, cold, fear, terror, pain, loneliness, they all are going to be tested on him, in following days, without any interval. The dance of death has started in the form of shock wave with emmense heat that will burn to ashes, anything which comes in its way. Our heartbeat had increased. We had locked ourselves in the fort, the only vision we could see was through cc camera with microphone, in our moniter. Outside a pindrop silence indicated, a storm of terror developing. Two hours passed without any disturbance. We were in doubt of fear, then understood that himalyan heights had blocked the shockwave. No way, we could go outside and investigate. After five hours, we saw some disturbance, Sudenly the wind speed rose to heights, with dust and smoke. The dome became out of site and all hell broke loose. Temprature rose to maximum, fireballs began to fall every where, could hear shrieking voice, fortwall trembeling on impact. Terror stricken, we rushed to the basement, hiding below stone platform. For hours we sat there, without talking, without doing anything. It was five o clock in the morning, we felt some ease. Taking strength we all came up, finding everything in place felt some relief. Temprature has increased to eighyt degree celcius, we were all perspiring. Deep darkness outside, thumping of walls too had stoped, we could not understand the reason. After half an hour the same havoc started and again we rushed to basement. Gauri explained this, said bhaiya, big tornados have developed and in the center there is zero activity that we had felt a little while ago, then again the outer pressure. These tornados suckup even big houses from root, our dome was very light in weight, we will not see it again. Tears began to roll from Tanya's eyes. What happened to our food stock and other things, stored in basement? Lost in thoughts of misery, we sat there for hours, without thinking of hunger and thirst. We had taken too much pains, in erecting that dome has gone with the wind at its first stroke. If we too had been there, what would have happened, we could not imagine. We thanked God that we were safe here in fort. After twenty hours Gauri forced us to eat, some dry fruits, salted mixture and water, saying, it will strengthen our morale. After drinking water we felt better. It became necessary to be more vigilant so we started our daily routine. For three days the disturbance of wind, converting into storm, trees, stones, hitting fort walls and natures fury, continued. With shaking hands we performed our duties. In worshiping too, we could not consontrate. We began to think that if, four thousand km away from the Dragon clutches, protected by himalyan ranges, we are suffering this much, how much difficulties, neibouring contries poor people will be bearing? It was unimaginable. The tornado continued fourth night, when Gauri woke up from sleep crying. She was repeatedly saying, I have seen a terrible dream that we all are throne into a storm and are flying and crying for life. We were in peril and hearing this all became frightend. The dogs too were barking. It was a bad sign so we decided to check everything around us. Raju and Juli were in security duty. He said that at night he had heard something falling but could not find it. Taking our torches we checked outside wall and saw a cement plaster missing and a crack from top to bottom.. Minutely checking cracks were found in many places, It meant the front wall had become unstable and will go down on further impact. Shocked to the bone, we stud still and silently shifted our belongings to the basement, including fanturbine and bulbs. There was no other way left for us. We were in trouble. There was not enough space, we could not movr around and the light bulb will not lost long without charging. Outside the disturbance started again. We sat there for twelve hours, peraspiring and did not have any courage left to go up and investigate. At last Raju took courage and asked my permission to go down from bottom door and open it to get some air. Prepared for emergency Raju took his backpeck and wearing helmet, he opend the door. The wind had stopped, in complete darkness. He pulled the rope, they had fastened between the dome and fort basement door, it was tight as before and in place. He exclaimed in surprise and cried, Amit da, I can not believe, it looks the dome is safe in its place. Why not take a chance? We have practiced many times. I want to go and look for the dome and the basement. It will take only fifteen minutes, and we may not get another chance. I had to agree with him. I said you may go but be carefull. Juli seconded his proposal but said she too will go with Raju. Two will be better than one and her training as swimmer and nursing will be helpful. It was agreed that they both Raju and Juli will go to search and come back immediately. I and Manish will hold the rope this side and wait for their signal, when they reach there. Embracing us, Raju and Juli inserted their hook in the rope and ran towords the dome and vanished in darkness. Tears in our eyes, we waited anxiously, for their signal of reaching safely. It seemed a long time. It was unbearable. It was decided that if it was safe, they will pull the rope twice otherwise pulling once they will come back. When fifteen minutes passd and no signal from Raju, I began to blame myself for sending Raju in danger. Sudenly the rope pulled once and we sighed with relief, saw Raju coming but alone. We were shocked to see him alone leaving Juli some where but when he told the good news we were over whelmed. Not only the dome was safe but Raju had left Juli there to help us getting in closed door. As decided Manish and gauri hooked themselves with rope and taking Ruby and Macho with her, ran towords dome Raju following. Tanya and I were ready properly hooked with rope, waiting for the signal and when it came, I started running pulling Tanya behind. Great patches of black dust had begun to fall on us. By the time, we reached the dome and were pulled inside the dome by Raju and Manish, we were soaked in black. Juli was smiling and everybody thanked Raju for his timely suggestion. Entangied in each other arms we were filled with joy. Almighty God has heard our appeal of distress but the danger was not over. Second attack of rains filled with dust and smoke has already started, which had soaked us in black. We can hear the sound of heavy rain falling on the dome. Immediately we took out the battery and manual charger from the basement and connected it to the center pole. Switching on the lights, we looked at each other in dismay. Dirty cloths, entangaled hair, unshaved beard and we all began to laugh. We have crossed our first hurdle, by the grace of God, safely. Two more were to be crossed and they too were not less than danger but more severe. Gauri reminded me about the mistake, we have done, in assessing the danger. From the begning we were talking about two shelters. First to save us from storm and shockwave at ground leval and second to save from heavy rains and flood at high leval but we have done the opposite. Looking to the fort as strong enough and to the dome, frail looking, we have done the blunder, which might have caused us with our life. By the grace of God, the basement at fort saved us. The same mistake, we were going to repeat again, living in low ground against heavy rains and flood. Will the God pardon us for this immature decision, we maid? I ran to the temple and standing on knee, started praying and asking forgive for my ill decision. Oh Almighty God, shri Brmha, shri Vishnu, shri Maheshwar, pardon me for my wrong decisions. For my mistake please do not punish my younger friends, who had always worshiped you and had done nothing wrong with others. Tears began to roll from my eyes in repentance.

I immediately engaged all of them in duty. Raju and Juli at observation post, Manish at manual battery charger, Tanya in radio and Gauri in preparing food, we have not tested in many days. From the beginning Gauri has played her part very well and all the credit goes to her only but being elder brother, I was lacking in my duties. Now it was my responsibilities that nothing should go wrong in future. What danger we were going to face was easy to access. Natures fury are attached together, after heavy rains, flood follow it. The astroid impact had increased it manyfold. The rains will continue upto the time till they are exhausted in removing their burden of smoke and vapour. Thinking al this in mind, I took a torch and started checking all the penals. Thumping eastside lower penals I heard heavy sound, it meant they are loaded with something, above I could see some dents too but otherside were light in sound. I decided in mind to check all the penals every four hours. Going to the observation post Raju informed me that the temperature had fallen a bit to seventy degrees and wind speed to three hundred km. ph. Falling rains were in many colors of black, red and yellow. It meant the upper atmosphere was full of them and was falling down. Tornado and rains were following each other. We were fortunate enough in running towords dome in the center of tornado. Switching on the search lights of observation post, when we looked out in tornado, we saw flying trees, stones, and veicles and in horror switched of the lights. It was very difficult to enalise, how much damage and change, those two asteroids

had made to the atmosphere. Every few minutes we heard
something hiting dome. There was only one consolation
that this dome has faced first impact very solidly and in
future too we will be safe. As usual, our daily routine of,
eating, drinking, sleeping in time started again but we could
not save us from the tension of being in danger, every second
of it. We had forgotten talking and laughing. For any small
impact we stoped doing, what we were doing at the time
and looked in suspence, heart beating running faster. Time
was forgotten. How much time had elapsed, nobody knew.
Only one thing was in our favour that we were doing our
jobs meticulously. Perhaps it was twelth day that Manish
informed that regular rains had started and is continuing.
The colour of rain water too looked changed and we could
see lightening every where and hear thundering of clouds.
It meant the second hurdle, we had crossed and the third
of flood will start soon. Ourbeard had grown, hairs were
entangaled. We had exhausted our supply of water pouch
and startedcollecting water from handpump. A slight
change in working was good for us, the monotonous went
away. We were worshiping daily but could not consontrate.
The rain was increasing every hour and the flood became
eminent, when we saw water siping from the main gate. We
saw an wood stick in between doors. Taking courage with
Manish I opened the gate, an air filled with stinking smell
flooded in, taking out the stick, we immediately closed the
door. The water was foaming with decayed materials. From
observation post, when we looked out, saw trees flowing
in water. Our farm was ten feet above the road, it means,
the full area was flooded with water. An inundation has
started and we can not reach at the height of fort. I can
not disclose my fear of drowning in the flood water. How

much water pressure this dome will bear, I did not know. Only God can help us. To boost up courage, I suggested full worshiping today evening, and everybody welcomed it. After many days suffering everybody looked happy and satisfied, as if they are getting something which had gone a miss. Hurriedly we bathed, changed cloths and collected in front of temple. We felt, as if we had done something wrong and were unable to accept. In between these past days, we have forgotten to worship collectively. Manish brought some flowers and Gauri started worshiping in traditional way singing Sanskrit shlokas. In Aarti, ringing bell and blowing horn, we chanted. Om jai jagdish hare, swami jai jagdish hare, bhkta janon ke sankat pal men dur karen, with full emotion. We accepted Prasad of sugar and coconut powder with humbleness. We were so much involved in worshiping that we did not hear any thumping sound or what is happening outside. All tention was gone, We felt, as if something we had lost, we have got it again. When Gauri served us salted potato chips and tetrapack milked tea, we were over joyed. Tears in her eyes Gauri began to say, God knows, what has happened to me, time passes but I culd not remember, what I have forgotten. From now on, we have to organize everything again and follow it strictly, then only we will achieve success. With determination we all started our daily routine, helping each other.

The most important job was at the observation post. The danger of flood was threatening us. Tornado and rains came one after another. Switching on the search lights, we recorded wind speed, air pressure, and calculated the flood leval. I checked all the penals and found solid sound indicating water leval at the height of eight feet, which was alarming. I was unable to judge the pressure dome will bear. After many days, I rememberd that Rampur and my house were submerged in flood water. What happened to my neibours, my near ones, I could not imagine. Tears filled my eyes. I felt sarrow for them. The feeling that this distruction had coverd whole of the earth shocked me. It must have changed the map of the world. On eighth day the sound of penals lessened. It means the flood leval is decreasing. I Felt relieved. I went to the post and tried to look out for any shadow of fort or side hill but could not see. Will the darkness prevail for months as predicted? I felt a shock in my heart. Will this disaster destroy human species from the earth, was a big question, nobody had an answer. Geologist had proved that in the beganing all the continents were united in one called Pangia. Earth's inner terbulance created tectonic plates, which moved upwords and in millions of year, the present continents came into existence. The question is whether in that time too these type of destruction happened? Strugaling and surviving man has prosperd. We too are strugaling. We could not count days and nights but with the help of clock, the time was moving ahead slowly, when Juli came running and informed that rain has stoped. We could not believe but we all rushed to the ob. post. We saw rain converted into grizele. We could see the shadow of fort a distance away. To show our gratitude to God, we had only one way, when we all bowed head worshipd. This was a special day, bathing and wearing fresh clothes, we assembled in front of temple. Today Gauri preached Satynarayan episode which surprised Tanya and Juli. Hindu mythology is full of them, which preach, peace, humanity, forgivness and duty. We all saluted God again and again and accepted Prasad of sugar and coconut powder as usual. We rememberd scientists warning that though our survival chances had increased but we were not out of danger. Still we had to cross many hurdules. One month had already passed but how many days more this condition will prevail, we did not know. When we will go out of this dome, it was not definite. If the God continued to give His support in future too, as He had given uptill now, we hope, we will cross all difficulties and will be able to worship Sun God too, out of the dome. The chance of hearing radio news from some where, were increased too. We might hear Geri's voice from space satellite, which was orbiting the earth. The radio became a source of inspiration for us. One of us was always busy tuning it. This expectation that the impct of Dragon is subsiding, our morale increased.

Our daily routine started as before, Yoga, exercise, bathing, and worshiping. Manish started teaching us growing plants and their maintainance. Every thing he had learned in college, he gave us lessons. Our future survival depends on it. We all took keen intrest on the subject. We must be selfsufficient in crop production. Third day Tanya called that she is receiving radio signal. Leaving all the work, we gatherd around the radio. At first some statice sound came than we heard Geri speaking in a low voice, I Geri Kerishkov speaking from orbiting capsule then radio became silent. We waited long time to hear more but no luck. For three continue days we tried to hear some thing but nothingcame out of it. On fourth day we heard Geri speaking fluently, For the second time, I came below black clouds to speak to you all, The condition has not decreased much, so I had to go upwords leaving you suddenly. Uper atmosphere is still coverd with black smoke. In some places it must be falling. I am going to tell you in short. Dragon's impact was so severe that to save myself from heated wave, had been a miracle of God who saved me. I was so busy in recording that I missed taking care of myself from danger approaching me. From Himalyan heights, the heat wave were coming towords me. Luckily I started my jet and went upwrds beyond the reach of smoke and heat. Whatever I see now is not hopefull. I could not see any fire but tornado are moving in some place. Heavy clouds are there and raining too. Millions tons of land and sea water has evouprated and they have collected here as clouds. Thet had to fall some where. Too much change had occurred in weather. For Gods grace you will be safe but be catious. Take care of your shelter and materials. This recording will be relayed every hour. Tomarrow I will speak to you again. You have crossed your first hurdle bravely. May God, help you. Thanks.

Geri Kerishkov's voice heard like God's voice from heaven. Lighted candle showing us the way. We had tears in our eyes for his greatfullness. An unknown man risking his life, sitting in a small capsule, hundreds of km above in the sky, guiding whole of the world, was encouraging us in everyway possible. We did not know, how much time he will be guideing us or when and how he will return to land, so in evening worshiping we prayed God to give him safe landing in time. Geri's voice filled us with new hope and energy and we began to plan our future working. It was definite that after these destructions, everything will be upsetdown. There will be no roads, no cities, only broken houses. To save ourselves, we will have to work hard, keep record of changing weather, and making new field to grow crop. Whatever stock of food and other things we have, they are more precious now till we would be able to grow them again. Most important question is whether in future, we can go searching people who had saved themselves and need help. On humanatarine ground we should do it first but in this condition, will it be possible? We all decided that this should be left in God's hand and we will do, what we can, in future.

Next day morning when we gatherd for breakfast on the dining table, everybody looked happy. Future planning was to be finalized. I asked for their suggestions, regarding possible difficulties and how to face them. Between us Raju and Juli had more experience of outside, so Raju suggested that first and foremost we should survey our surroundings and prepare our field for Manish, so that he could start sowing the crop as per weather. We should not think of going far from this place. Before this we should check our stock at fort and look after cows, we had left there. This sentence surprised us. In our own problems, we had totally forgotten about cows and calfs. Gauri, tears in her eyes said Oh God, how we had left them in hands of God, Can we go now and attend them? In this darkness, we can not see the fort even, then how could we reach there? There was only one answer. It is not proper, to put yourself in danger. Till the condition improves we had to leave them on God. Everybody was sad, we had to convince ourselves that they are safe upto this time, and will be safe for some more days. The time was five o clock in the evening and everybody was anixous to hear some new news from Geri Kerishkov. We could hear Geri speaking, clearly. He said friends, by Gods will, you will be safe. Today whatever I am going to tell you, nobody should bear this type of disaster twice. At the height of two hundred km above tibten platue, I was looking at my earth being destroyed. Looking how cruely that Dragon hit the earth. I had seen many times, this type of destruction by computer animation but in comparison of this teribaly spreading firestorm, they were nothing. Earths heart was torn to pieces and in reaction, earths lakhs of pieces jumped to the sky, to take revenge. The Dragan was destroyed in first impact but roaring in circles it was spreading all over to engulf the whole earth. Every where fire is burning and spreading. The hills wanted to stop it but invain. When Himalay wanted to stop, it advanced towords me shrieking. I was recording its dual part, which was hiting Atlantic Ocean, creating thousands of feet high tsunami waves to submerge nearby continents. Its heat had vaporized lakhs of tons of water, which were spreading in whole of the sky. Presing my heart I was looking at those two monsters united, making destruction in Europe and saw it advancing towords me. I had only one way to save myself so I took shelter in space. I could not dare to go again and watch. My whole body was trambeling. In our eyes we had helpless tears. At one side the darkness of space and another side below boiling dust and smoke. I felt sadness in my soul but when I looked at shining stars and moon, when in the morning felt sunrays energy flowing in me I felt as if they are consoling me that do not be dishearten. Like death life too is immortal. Once again the life will smle, flowers will blossom. When the darkness became less, it was confirmed that the God has ended Dragon forever. Taking courage to help and assist you in future strugules, today and every morning, to show and guide you, I will be available to you. God blessings are with us. Thanks.

Geri Kerishkov's massage that he will be guideing us in future made us happy. It was not easy to survey surrounding area without any guidance. All over the world, people were, listening this massage, will be benifited in locating safe place for their survival. In absence of facilities, they were acostomed to, every day they will face new problems, which was going to be nerve breaking. Who ever was prepared for this in advance, will cross the hurdle others will suffer to the extreme. Every day we waited for evening massage from Geri, heard his encouraging speech and wait for next day. Seven days passed without any change in weather condition. We were anxious enough in going to the fort, to look after the cows but outside, it was extremely dark. The air was polluted outside. We had to clean it by using our exhast fan filters, morning and evening. We were so busy in our daily routine that our beard has grown too much, for the lack of time. Gauri, Tanya and Juli had their hairs entangaled. They were doing their work honestly but their face showed fatigue. We had enough water to drink but for bathing we got only one bucket, every week. Other days we sponged ourselves. Knowingly we had made these arrangements to value the need of water and save it going waste. Our dress too had changed, we were in baniyain and halfpant, girls were in gown only. Neither we had time to wash clothes nor water to clean them. To adjust ourselves in this living condition, Gauri had made these strict rules and we were following it. As per our logbook this was our forty fifth day of suffering on twenty second february when Geri raised our hope, informing the upper ionosphere covered in black decreasing but below it the clouds boiling as before. He said to inform further development after few days as he is facing fuel shortage. We felt disappointment but the hope increased, that the weather will improve soon and we will be able to see SunGod. It was the last day of February that Manish and Gauri informed us that the temperature has gone down by five digree and wind speed too deceased, when I with Tanya were going to the post for duty. After an hour, we could see in some distance. We switched on the search light and moved it towords fort. We were shocked to see front two rooms, where we lived, fallen to the ditch below. If we had not moved in time, we all had died. The dream of Gauri and suggestion of Raju saved us by the grace of God. This change in weather indicated that day by day it will improve and we will be able to survey our surrounding area. Manish was excited, he said Dadu you wait and see, how early I will chnge it in greenery as before. How should I make him understoond that to devlope this land, become barren, to grow anything without sunlight will be impossible. Plants get energy from sun and the weather cicle depands on sun. In the evening Geri confirmed that the blackness has decrased and he could see some light above. The intensity of clouds too has gone less. It was a probability that the temperature will rise again which will invite rains afterwords. After that only it will be possible for Sun God to show his miracle in transforming the earth in greenery. Geri said, he will try to describe what and how all that happened in different place. What you have to do and where to go I will guide you. Till that time you might have sufferd more but keep faith on God, do not try to do anything in hurry. The last atacke and if you succeseed, you will get enough time to do and to show your worthiness. You may be able to give courage and chance to your coming generation. After so many days of suffering and waiting, Geri's encouraging words filled us with strength and joy.

We all decided that before the rains start again, not careing for darkness, we should see and try to go to the fort, to look after the cows and check our stock of food and other materials. We were in need of some rest so we cancelled our night watching, to have some more energy on day time. After months Gauri, Tanya and Juli prepared our dinner enthusiastically. We have forgotten the taste of vegitabels, which had exhausted in early days but the spinach, which Manish had grown in nursery tasted very good. Tention free dinner gave us a good sound sleep after many days and we woke up at six in the morning. Eagerly we bathed and collected infront of Temple. Today we were going to enter in danger zone so it was a special worshiping. We all traditionally worshiped one by one and combined together did Havan, a special offering to God. Accepting Prasad we three, Me RAju and Manish wearing raincoat, mask, helmet, taking torch, two bags full of food for cows and shovel, became ready to go to the fort. Gauri, Tanya and Juli were looking at us in fear. They had to close the door immediately after. The search lights were on. We tightened a rope at the gate and hooked ourselves in it, When we opened the door a stench welcomed us but holding the first rope left there, we went forword in darkness, shining torch we could see first rope under deep mud. Neglecting it we moved stumbling towords fort direction. The basement door was full of stone and mud. We cleared it by shovel and opened the door. Withgreat pleasure we found all thefoodstuff and material safe. To open the stone block we three had to use our full strength in removing it, but we were successful. Cowdung smell was every where. The cows and calves looked thin. We cleaned them with water, collected by rains and fed them with food, salt and rawsugar, we had brought. We arranged the fodder left over and returned back, closing the stone block and basement door. The rain had already started as predicted by Geri. Our cows were safe but did all innocent animals, beasts and birds survived. It was a big question and nobody had an answer. That day passed happily In the evening Geri informed hopefull news. The density of blackness above clouds belowhas decreased. Tropical areas were still in rainstorms. Geri told some confusing information. He has read that in every twenty thousand year, the iceage returns. Had that time passed? The scientist resurch show that only fifteen hundred year are left in coming of that time and the process may start from now. Unusual rain, flood and snow storms are happening every year, may be a prior indication of iceage. Has this Dragon impact, trigerd the happening more. If so, people will have to be moved towords equator. Saying is easy but can that be done to billions of people? Be prepared for that too.

We all were listening, Geri speak in dumb silence. Tanya began to shade tears, saying we faced this problem every year in Russia. We could save ourselves from cold but it was very difi cult to arrange food in that cruel weather. We did some hunting too but after this when all wild animals will be killed, what will happen, I do not know. How my country people will survive, I can not imagine. I am glad that mummy, papa and sister are safe and are trying to reach here, which is safe enough and near to equater. Hearing Tanya talking like this, we too were sadend. Sudenly we heard crackaling sound and rushed to the obs. post, switched on the search lights and saw hailstorm. Outside everything looked white. We had just heard Geri talk about it and the devil has come in a new form. In reality if, what Geri has said, is going to be true, it is going to be a great blow to humanity and it may wipe out some of the species, forever. Again we started four hours duty of checking from observation post. Night passed very worriedly. Next day morning, when we gatherd around dining table, for breakfast, we started discussing about the problem of iceage, which Geri had said it to become a reality. At first we searched in books. We could only find that it is a natural finomina, which is repeated in time again and again, by nature. From north and south pole, the snow accumulate in huge quantity and form glashiers. These glashiers flow down and create rivers, vallies and lakes in summer heat. These changes are made in hundreds of year, has already happened thousands of time in past and will happen in future too. In earth histry of billions of year, north and south poles have changed their position too, which may be a reason of forming iceage. Sun's sour storms too can help in making iceage. Gauri continued speaking, she said, this time two incident happened at a time, first the astrid impact which rose the temperature manyfold by heatwave and second tsunami waves created by second asroid, which increased the vapour quantity in atmosphere, which resulted heavy rains through out the earth. We can not predict the effects it had made in the invoiranment now. In future, we will the results it had made but they are going to be a sevsre one. I am not botherd about iceage because it will not happen in one day. It will take many years gradually forming ice, gradually advancing towords equator. At present, we should do, what we have been doing till now. We were astonished listening Gauri talking about his general knowledge of every subject gained by books and internet. We all agreed to her proposal. Gauri said everybody should know all the jobs, we do in our home, so from today man will prepare food and his partner will guide him. I and manish knew nothing about cooking and Raju knew only making omelette, tost and tea but the suggestion was good so we all agreed. Second thing which Gauri said seemed to be a difficult one. She said our ancestors in primitive era kne, how to make fire with the help of wood sticks, so it will be better to learn it, in case of exhausting our matchbox stock. Tanya And Juli embraced Gauri immediately saying, Gauri Didi how could you remember all these minor things, which can be so important in future. We care and engage ourselves in todays work, what of tomarrow. Gauri replied Bhabhi ji nothing new I had said, if you think of tomarrow, you will get the same answer. Now, we should not waste time, today Mani will prepare food and I will guide him. At night Amit da and tomarrow morning Raju bhaiya with his patner will do the job. This competition made us more active in mind in thinking new ideas. Days began to pass easily. From morning to afternoon we were busy doing our work but in the evening we enjoyed very much by singing, playing games, telling stories about past happenings and Geri speaking. At night we discussed on important subjects as what we will do if, the darkness prevaild for many more months, if the nearby land became mudfilld by heavy rain, if we had to go from here, where we will go and how, if the crop we grew, was destroyed, what will we eat. This type of questions were asked and we tied to suggest answers. Everybody took part in discussions and we were astonished to know that everybody rememberd the answer. Gauri always said if ther is a problem, its answer is there too. This was true also. We continued discussing and found the solution too. We began to underatand that if we had to go out, leaving this dome, we will have to wander here and there like nomads, will have to search new place for living, will have to bear thirst and hunger. These discussions made us strong in facing coming difficulties, inspired our will to conqer them.

The rains were continueing. Once in a week, we went to the fort and took care of the cows. Whenever we went, the dogs Ruby and Macho accompanied us. They smelled in ground and barked. We understood that creatures living underground were more active. The masquitos and flies were in increasing number. Days were passing uneventfully now when on thirtieth March Geri informed a change in clouds below, where he was able to see a glimps of our earth. He spoke gladly that that upper blackness had diminished and clouds below looked white now. It was a clear indication that very soon we were going to worship Sun God. We all were rocking together in happiness. We had crossed three months of suffering. Even one day looked heavy on us. Embracing each other, we were praising God. At seven pm we were worshiping with devotion and requesting God, as he had saved us, he must have saved billions of people, animals, birds and trees around the world. But we had a fear in our heart that what are wegoing to see outside? How early we would see our people laughing and singing? How early we would see animals feeding green grass and birds flying and singing in the sky?

The night passed very quickly, expecting a new morning. Gouri woke all of us and in mirror showed our face. Seeing him or herself looked bewilderd. We three men had whiskerd and hairs grew like primitive men, Tanya and juli's bobed hairs had grown to entangaled long tail. For the first time we laughed together seeing each other. Gouri brought out shaving kit, scissor, blade and requested us to look ourselves presentable. All were eager but nobody knew the art of hair cutter. Juli came saying she had some knowledge of cutting, learned in nursing training. She never got chance to do it but she can try. Raju brought his mobile phone and took many photographs for future rememberance, in group and in pairs. One by one Juli shortened hairs and whiskers byscissor, then shaving became easy. She and Tanya applied the same technique and cut their hairs as before. Gauri applying oil on hairs made them look good. After taking bath and wearing fresh cloths, we were filled with joy. Raju again took photographs and were loaded in laptop. These small acts were to entertain us, to remind us, our sufferings bore in last three months and were going to give new energy, to face against coming difficulties in future. After worshiping and Aarti we assembled for breakfast and decided to survey the outside surroundings to make our future action plan. We all prepared ourselves with backpeck, raincoat, and mask. All search lights were on and what we saw outside made us despair, immobile. The beautifull tank was converted into an uneven ground, the side road was filled to the top with stones, fort side ditch was full with fallen fortwall stones and whwn we looked at the temple hill on east side, it has vanished. Shaken to the bone, we could not see more, came back hurriedly inside. The feeling that how God has saved us, in these happenings, jolted us. Dumbfounded we all sat in front of our small temple before God Bramha, Vishnu, Maheshvara, bowed head praying. We could not request Him for anything. We could not ask Him for pardon, HE had given us all HE could, by giving us a new life. He had given us a boon which nobody had heard in stories.

Going outside, made us realize that unless all the conditions improve, we should wait here and do not think about going out. Geri was helping us as a guide and we should follow his instructions strictly. Earnestly, daily routine started again. Every morning and evenng went to the observation post in the hope to see daylight but came back disappointed. Daily heard Geri speaking. Again and again, a thought disturbed us that we living here safely feel so much suffering and tention, what about those, who were compaled to live in temporary shelter, would be feeling. Our heart trembled with fear. After many days the rain stopped. We could see fallen fort walls in day time. We could not see them in night. We could differenciate in day and night but we could not dare to go outside. We were safe here and had enough stock of every thing we needed. Going out side, we will have to face new chalanges and to do more labour, Gauri made some chages in routine. Both the time, nutrisous food was given to every one, more sports, Yoga and exercises were utilized to gain strength. All the window penals were opened. Manish began teaching, growing plants, crops and vegetables, every evening. Juli started giving firstaid training. We all slept soundly at night. Eighth day Geri gave the new hopefull information that following daylight, he had seen some spots of earth and some greenery at equater. He could not contect to his base camp. Traveling a lot, searching, he is short in fuel and will have to land somewhere soon. Through GPS he is trying to search a safe place to land, where he could get some help in saving himself but it seems imposible. Please note my satellite phone number. +88169918827734 and try to contect me. The dificulti is that I know only Russian and few words of English, perhaps your support will provide me a safe landing and will be meeting you with open heart. Thank you very much. Hearing the massage and satellite phone noumber Tanya began to dance looking happy and saying oh God please help me in talking with Geri. If I can talk to him, he will talk with papa and I will get the information of papa being safe some where. Please God, I will worship you daily, please, please. She had tears in her eyes for gratefulness. We too were with her. At night worshiping we all were hopefull and full of expectation that God will fulfill Tanya's wish. Geri's news that all has not ended, men will again strugule and will be able to prosper again by his wisdom and knowledge, made us happy. Tanya, many times a day tried to contact Geri but failed. We did not know, how many communication satellite were destroyed in this violent wind. Normaly every day more thn two hundred lightening erupted on earth that disturbed communication but at present, they were more and every where. We had to convince Tanya that there is no harm in trying and sending Uncle Terishkov's number in Russian, again and again. Geri's message was relayed for many days, Fourth day Geri said about a number being transmited him in Russian but he could not follow it completely. He was thankfull to the person, who had sent him the number and will try to contact. He further said that that the temperature has gone down and everybody should be prepared for cold and make arrangements to light fire. I want that tomarrow night at seven, everybody start fire or lightening. We will get two advantages from it. First I will be able to ascertain, where people had been saved and still living and secondly, you too will, be aware of nearby surroundings, where people are safe and waiting to be contected in getting or giving help. After that I will decide to land safely. This novel idea of Geri filled us with hope and energy. As before Tanya was busy with satellite phone, hoping if the weather is clear she mighi send or receive message. Next day at seven in the night, we arranged to light up a huge fire outside of dome. Gauri suggested that every year we used to celibrate Holi festival in the monthof Falgun that is march then why not we celibrate it, and worship, in that way. The sacred fire burning will enlighten our soul, keeping all miseries away and give proper signal to Geri too. At five in the evening, collecting all empty boxes, when we opened the gate, we began to trembale in cold breeze. Lighting all the search lights, we collected boxes and used up papers Gauri arranged all worshiping materials, like flowers, rice, chandan sicketc and fifteen minutes before started worshiping, remembering devotee Prahlad and God Narsinha. We all joined in prayers and ignited the fire. Fire started furiously in cold breeze and we all were moving around in circle celibrating Holi festival. We were dancing and singing around it, like we did in campfire. We were full of hope and new found energy. We tried to look far away for any light or fire but we could not see anything. We might had seen from the fort height. We did not know weather Geri saw it or not but flies began coming in flocks and we had to run inside for safty.

Next day evening Geri announced the encouraging news that he had seen lights in some place of equater contries. The weather is improving fast, clouds too are thinning. It is expected that sun may rise soon. No improvement near northpole is seen. Nobody knows when the nature will change its behavior. Some days back scientist were worried about increasing population, air pollution, global warming and vanishing glaciers but nature, at a stroke, has changed it. She has warned us that extreme of anything is not good. Uptill we will be following natural rules, there will be peace and happiness in the world. The sudden improvement in weather indicates that fear of iceage, God has advanced ahead. I have to enquire about a signal received from 35digree latitude and 80 digree longtitude, some where near Afganistan and India border. Every day now I see the Sun God. You too are proceeding from darkness to light. I wanted to stay here for some more days but going up and down, wandering here and there had consumed more fuel and I have to land soon. Let the God decide, I meet some one who accept me as a family member, when I land on the ground. I Geri Kerishkov, will serve you for three, four days more then Gods will.

The iceage formula had disheartened us but Geri's encouraging words had changed it altogather and we were dancing with pleasure. The satellite signal Geri was talking abou, seemed to be near uncle Terishkov direction. Was it possible that Geri was asking about the same signal? Tanya was asking the same question from everybody, again and again. Perhaps God has heard Tanya's appeal. On next days announcement gladly Geri made it clear saying, I contected the satellife number, sent by an unknown person, which happened to be of my own countryman Mr. Terishkov. He had promised me to guide, for a safe landing of my capsule. I was able to understand the number in many repeatition. Who ever had sent me that number, I thank him or her, with gratitude. If God will permit me, I surely will come there to pay my respect. The condition is improving day by day. If you are in trouble then only you come outside. Without the help of rope or any person do not try. Still there is a possibility of rain and heavy wind. Try to hear radio news, you may get some help or news from your government. Thanks.

Tanya was convinced that her papa, mummy and sister were safe. She had received Karu's treasure was her feeling. Bowed head, standing on knees, tears in her eyes, she was praying in front of temple before Almighty God. We were glad but astonished. Doings of God are unimaginable. Her minor efforts have given her great achievement. At Gita,

Lord Krishna had satd, karmanye vadhikaraste ma faleshu kadachanam. It meant, Do your duty without wishing any results. And after some days Gauri saw a thin shining light appearing from east. We ran outside and with bowed head, both hands clasped together in front, looked, emerging from darkness, Sun God. Tears in our eyes, praying, again and again,

Tamso Ma Jyotirgamay
Oh God Please Lead Me To Light From Darkness.

'The End'

Printed in the United States
By Bookmasters